Books by Reneé Porter

Bell Park
Dreamville

The Taliaferro Chronicles
The 13th Victim
Redemption Ridge
An Inquisition of Angels

An Inquisition of Angels

Volume III of

The Taliaferro Chronicles

Reneé Porter

Roet Press   Plantation, Florida

DEDICATION

For Rob, my True North

Bequest

You left me, sweet, two legacies, -
A legacy of love
A Heavenly Father would content,
Had He the offer of;

You left me boundaries of pain
Capacious as the sea,
Between eternity and time,
Your consciousness and me

                    Emily Dickinson

Chapter One

Her last, sweet breath was what he waited to inhale. That was their true moment of communion, the joining of their souls as he touched her lips with his and waited to breathe deeply.

The last breath was sometimes so fast that he had missed it a few times with other angels. It had taken practice and precision on his part to coordinate everything that preceded the pressing and that last exhalation from their sweet lips.

Though the tight, saw-toothed iron collar prevented the angels from screaming or even speaking, it did not prevent that last, albeit short, thread of air from slipping from between their lips. And tonight it had gone perfectly. He inhaled deeply as the mortal life of the angel passed into his body.

Their lives had become his from the moment he had first spied them running on the trail of eastern Orlando's Cady Way Park. People used it throughout the day and into the early evening, but it was such a large trail that it provided him endless points to capture his angels. From its northern trailhead, it wound through residential areas, old railways, and through the deserted military base at its southern regions.

For him, it was the perfect place of communion. Developed by the city, God had led him to the park. Why God would choose this location for his angels to appear was unknown to the man. But, because the isolation of certain parts of the seven mile path, the man had his choice of places to hide and wait for an angel to appear. Sometimes he had to wait several weeks before he saw her; but, once he did, he began the process of planning her capture and taking her to his home in the rural area between Orlando and the east coast of Florida.

The angel he had pressed tonight had been the easiest to capture. When he first saw her moving along the path, he knew that she was one of God's chosen. The man believed that only the holiest of women would dare to tread alone on this path to which God had directed him.

There were always prerequisites to be met before he took an angel. God had given him many commandments and rules to which he had to adhere or risk the Lord's displeasure. Thus, he researched each angel's life as part of his preparation. Her physical appearance was not enough, but she must be pale white without any blemishes and her hair had to be a shade of red, although God had given him permission to take some blondes if their other attributes were acceptable, but their hair had to have its natural color. Physically, she had to be perfect as he knew heaven would allow no angel to disguise itself otherwise.

There were other requirements, especially her Christian name. She had to have a holy name given to her at birth and it had to appear in the King James Version of the Bible, but that left him a wide selection of names. She could have no children, although virginity was not required. He knew that the angels might allow the temptations of their mortal form to fall to such weaknesses and so that was not required.

The angel he had completed his tasks with tonight always ran the same route every weeknight and she always chose a time when few, if any other runners, were out. He had watched her for two weeks before acting. As she passed his hiding spot behind a hedge of red hibiscus blooms bordering the path, he could almost see the glow of her body nearing him, her transparent wings, visible only to him, propelling her forward.

He loved to see the flight of the angels down the path and it increased his anticipation of the moment when he would take each angel's heavenly essence into his being. His steps for an angel's capture were simple. He had found that any intricate snares could cause him great trouble and had cost him a few angels over the past few years. What he did was so simple that no traces of the angel or his presence were ever found.

He waited weeks for the right time and then just as the angel approached his hiding place among the fragrant blooms, if it was safe and no one else was about, he would jerk a heavy line of monofilament fishing line upward from where it lay on the path with the other end tied tightly to a distant tree.

As the angel tripped and began to fall, he would rise from the darkness of the green bushes, his great shape enveloping her wings around her body and he would pull her over the hedge and into his strong arms, smothering her mouth and nose with chloroform laced cotton quilt batting he had found in his family's old home. Each angel never had time to register what had happened before the strength of the chloroform would render her silent and motionless.

He would wait once more, watch the path, and quickly carry the angel's mortal body to the trunk of his sedan. There he had already placed lengths of duct tape hanging on the inside of the trunk lid. He had the duct tape placed in the needed order, from the shorter length for her mouth to the longer strips for binding her limbs. If no one were nearby, he would use the tape on her hands, feet, and mouth and shut the lid. If people were drawing close to the car or coming down the path, they would see nothing but a man leaning against the back of his car, dressed for running and bent over as if trying to stretch his limbs after a long run.

To the average passerby, there seemed nothing memorable about him as no one could see his size or face because of the way he would be positioned as they passed, usually with the front of his body facing the trunk.

Once they were gone, if they ever were there, he would then return to retrieve the monofilament and use a palm frond or a convenient branch to sweep his existence away from the site. It usually took him at least 15 minutes to remove all traces of his angel and himself from the park and another 20 minutes to drive to his house, just outside Christmas, Florida. He used the drive time to mentally tick off his list of completed tasks to ensure that he had forgotten nothing.

The simpler, the better, he had learned and that thought made him smile, knowing that he and his angel would be safe from the mortals who walked in sin around them each day.

The first thing he did upon his arrival home was to take his angel to the old hunting cabin that had been built on his property long before his family had erected their house there. The cabin sat back deep in the woods beyond the pool and would be unseen by anyone at the rear part of his lawn.

He kept his property immaculate, with a well manicured lawn, flowering shrubbery, and a few citrus trees. He made friends with distant neighbors by offering them some of the fruit from his trees and visited them at times in order to keep them away from his home. He attended church with many of them each week and was involved with the activities of his church as long as those activities did not interfere with his work with the angels.

But he was disgusted by those people and their foul, sinful bodies. He had to scrub his body after each time he was near them. Their vile mortality made him sometimes aware of the building poisons in his body and so he would scrub and scourge his body to rid their taint from him.

If they had come to his home, which they seldom if ever did, they would never have found one of his angels. By that time, the angels were enduring the tests he had to perform to make sure that each one was the angel he thought her to be.

Sometimes he had more than one angel at a time. The process of purification and their testing was lengthy and if one failed, he would begin again with the second or third one. He had room for four angels, but he had never had more than three at any one time.

After stripping them of their human clothing, he would leave their pure, angelic forms as God had placed them on this earth. He examined their bodies for any imperfections and reveled in the glory of the beauty God had given them.

They were soundless when they awoke because he began their first test after undressing them by placing an iron collar around their throats. He had made all his tools himself, studying the intricacies of the devices from drawings and in one instance, from an actual antique device in a museum. He took a blacksmithing class and a welding class at schools distant from his home and had learned the rudimentary principles he needed to make small, crude items that would give no one cause to see his true proficiency, which was necessary to do as God had commanded.

Each collar was heavy iron that made it impossible for the angels to raise their heads unassisted or else their necks would snap. Each collar, rusted by time and many uses, was finished with sharp saw teeth that dug into their lower jaw and neckline, making it impossible for them to open their mouths beyond a small parting of their lips without the saw teeth cutting their throats.

The collar was the first of the tests and if he had more than one angel, he knew that they psychically communicated to one another not to scream or try to talk. If they accepted that they could not speak or call out and survived for seven days without dying, they passed the first test.

He would begin the second test once the seven day period of wearing the collar would end.

As they were heavenly creatures only appearing in mortal form, at first he did not think that he needed to feed them or give them water, even when the temperatures inside the cabin would soar well past 100 degrees, especially during the hot Orlando summers. But after he had lost a few angels to dehydration, he realized that their human form was a crutch to which he had to administer and so he did give them water daily as necessary, though he saw no need for food. They were healthy and strong in their mortal forms when he took them and the lack of food might weaken them, but he decided it would not kill them.

The second test was the strappado. He would carry them to the center of the cabin and gently lie their naked bodies on the rough wooden floor. He would roll them onto their bellies and take a long leather strap, attach one end to their wrists tied behind their backs and the other thrown over a rafter in the cabin.

Lifting them to a standing position and removing the collar, he would gag them with old rags. He would then use a winch to raise their arms upward from behind them, often either dislocating their shoulders or breaking their arms. The pain from this test was unbearable, but the only relief he gave them was the removal of the collar. The rags were meant only to make their screams inaudible.

He would leave them hanging for seven hours and then lower their torn bodies to the ground and placing the collar once more on their fragile necks. He would do this each night for seven days.

On the second night, he would enter and give them water, repeat his ritual, help them to their feet and lean them against the post in the cabin, warning them that if they fell, the pain of being lifted by the strappado would be worse.

He quoted scripture to them as he performed the test of the strappado each night, describing their position within the pantheon of heaven and how the Lord would welcome them back among his fold, their tasks upon the earth completed.

The third test, ducking, was almost as simple as the collar, although he did not need to fabricate any device for the ducking. He once more removed their collars, led them through the woods to his backyard and simply threw their bodies into his swimming pool. He would leave their arms untied as they were useless, broken limbs. The only way they could survive the ducking was to use their legs to propel them upward. If he saw them surface. he would wade into the water, quote the testament of John the Baptist, praising mighty God for the salvation of their angelic souls, and help them through the deeper water until their feet could touch the bottom of the pool. They were then forced to walk out of the pool and back to their space in the cabin and once more the collar was placed on them. They would be tested six more nights in this manner before passing this test.

By this time, most of them barely had the strength to walk so he rarely worried about securing their legs to keep them from running away, but once, one of the stronger angels had used this time to try and run from his house. The first time it had happened he had been totally unprepared and had chased her across his front lawn before catching up to her and tackling her to the ground.

Unfortunately, in her weakened condition, the tackle had snapped her weak neck when she fell and he knew then that he could not allow the useless loss of another angel, much less risk the chance that they might be seen.

He then had made chains for their feet and had grasped their broken arms tightly as he led them to the pool. Once there, he would sit them upon the stone wall, the very stones that would later be used for the pressing, and remove the chains from their feet. Then it was an easy movement of pushing them into the deep end of his pool and leaving their survival to their holiness in the eyes of the Lord.

And while most of them did survive the first three tests, some of them did not. Not all of them had been angels. Some of them had failed the tests long before the final test and the release of pressing. They were merely mortal women, impure and unclean.

It was the fourth test, the Pear, that proved to him and the Lord that they were truly angelic creatures. It was also the worst of the tests for it involved the insertion of a pear shaped metal object into their female orifice. A device he had discovered in his research of Inquisition techniques, it was devastatingly deadly. He would hang them with the strappado again, place the gags in their mouths and slowly raise them into the air where their legs twitched as they swung in the air.

He would steady their bodies, find their sex and then gently insert the Pear inside them. After the insertion, the device would be opened slowly into razor sharp leaves that expanded and shredded their interior mortal tissue by way of a winding button that he twisted at the base of the Pear. As the leaves expanded, the leaves would also twist with each turn of the screw. The unfortunate consequence of the removal of the device, however, would also usually remove their outer genitalia. He was not sure that the original device was intended to do this, but he felt that it must have been a divine effect of the device he had made as it left the angels unsexed and as he had read in many ancient texts, angels were without sex.

This was the only test he performed once. If they survived the Pear and did not bleed out during the night, they had proven themselves to be the heavenly creatures he needed and they were ready for the pressing.

He had been confused when he was younger as to how to capture and test his angels. He knew that every action he performed, every word spoken to them, had to have a holy meaning. He believed that he was chosen by God to return these wandering angels to heaven.

He studied Biblical texts and histories for many years before devising the sequence of the techniques he needed to use to test them first. He had surprisingly found them in texts describing the tests used by the Inquisition to prove witchcraft. That was when he had found his answer and it had made him laugh. He thought the inquisitors to be fools.

Of course they had failed to find real witches. Witches were a human mythology, created by men to punish recalcitrant or defiant women and heretical men. Yes, he thought, that was why they had failed. He thought of the real angels they might have destroyed needlessly and it angered him. They were searching for diabolic women. They should have been seeking angels.

And the angel he had now was pure until the end. She had survived each test – the collar, the strappado, the ducking, and finally the pear. When she had lived through the pear, the most devastating of the tests, he knew that she was pure and divine. He had taken her body, washed each inch of it tenderly, and swaddled it completely in the purest of white cotton. He had carried the angel, still wearing the collar, to his pool side and lay her body upon a black plastic tarp. He then had placed the pressing board upon her body, leaving only the collar and her head uncovered.

He had brushed and spread her long hair out to form a halo flowing outward from her head. Sometimes the women were awake during this final portion of his worship and tears would flow copiously from their eyes as he began placing the pressing stones upon their chests. The collar and swaddling cloth prevented any movements and their faces were always facing upward as he prepared them for their heavenly ascension.

This angel had been one of the most beautiful of all the ones he had taken. With each stone he placed, he kissed the tears from her eyes. The collar had prevented any sound but the deepest of moans and he knew when she was close to her rising as the weight of the stones pushed her tongue out of her mouth. The tongue was engorged and served to further block her ability to breathe. It was when the tongue appeared that he placed his mouth over hers and drew out that last breath and grasped his own member to expel the poisonous demon fluids that had built up within himself that could only be released with the thrust of her tongue into his mouth as her mortal form released her last breath.

Afterwards, he had lain next to her for several hours, and sometimes had to release more poison from his own body again by taking her upthrust tongue into his mouth and sucking it as his body was cleansed. When he finished each time, he believed he saw the ethereal form of her angelic body as it was transported upward, watching him from the star filled sky.

When he, too, finally felt completely clean and pure once more, he began the disposal of her mortal remains. He took the long, flat pressing stones and placed them back into the stone wall around the pool first, and then took the black plastic drop cloth and wrapped her crushed and stained mortal envelope in it and carried the human carcass to the woods beyond his home where he had dug a hole for her remains many nights before he had captured her.

He had two areas where he placed the remains. The angel he had just allowed to ascend would go to the area where her sister angels' bodies resided. What better choice for their remains than a place called Christmas? He had known that this was to be his place to serve the Lord even as he had grown up there.

If the chosen one had proven to be merely a mortal woman, a fallen mortal woman who had failed his tests, he would drive her out away from his home to outside another nearby town called Bithlo and toss the body into a swamp where he had weighed the body down with stones. He would roll it into the deep black water there and watch it sink into the brackish water. He carried a gun with him on those trips as the alligators, the serpents who might feed on his own purity, sometimes ventured out.

But not tonight, the glorious angel with the red and blonde hair had given him the freedom of saving his immortal soul from any serpent. That her name was Martha made the experience the holiest of holies for him.

Chapter Two

Pea sat on the front steps of their home in Staunton, Virginia and watched as her twin sons and her niece chased the bubbles she blew outward toward them. The three toddlers giggled and ran in circles trying to capture the sunlit bubbles that the soft summer breeze moved around and upward.

She smiled as she watched them. Ree's daughter, a curly haired blonde, was almost four months older than Pea's boys, but she was more like her aunt Pea and often stood to the side as Trey's dark haired boys would point out the bubbles she should chase.

The boys were very verbal for their age and though they had never really developed the twin-speak that some twins had, they did have some sort of silent communication with one another that involved the simplest of gestures, from a raised eyebrow to a shoulder shrug. Those gestures reminded her so much of Trey that it made her ache even though he was never very far away from any of them.

The past three years might have destroyed many couples. From Manley to the New River killers, they had somehow managed to not only survive the outside forces that literally had tried to kill them, but they had survived the psychological toll such traumas take upon most couples.

Ree and Joseph had found their bond just as strong and had come to stay with Pea and Trey in Staunton rather than going back to the rebuilt farm in Greenbrier County. There were ghosts in both places for all of them, but Ree told Pea once in confidence that she never felt safe at her childhood home after "the ridge" and though she tried to stay there, she knew that she needed to be away from there. Pea was unsurprised by this revelation on her sister's part as Ree was always finding excuses to stay at the Staunton farm.

Ree, who had always been fearless, now seemed to be unable to leave the family that she, Pea and their husbands and children had formed. Joseph never complained. One day he simply packed their bags, loaded their Volvo station wagon, and drove his family to Staunton. He made arrangements for personal items to be moved and never looked back. As always, for Joseph, Ree and his daughter were his only concern.

Everyone had begun to call Mary "Ree", except for Joseph during certain moments. Three years ago she would have bristled at the use of the childhood nickname. Now it gave her a sense of comfort and family that she welcomed gladly. She never talked about practicing law anymore or even opening a small practice in Staunton. When Joseph broached the subject with her, he was ignored and informed that she was too busy raising their daughter to think about taking the bar exam.

Events had not been so good for Thomas and Diana, either. Thomas had come home shortly after Pea had given birth to the boys to find that Diana had packed and left to go back to Baltimore, leaving him only a short note that said, "I love you, but I can't do this. I'm sorry."

Thomas had called to make sure that she had arrived safely and that she was okay, but he had not asked her to come back. He knew she could not compete with the ghost of Shawnette and she had given up trying although Thomas never spoke of Shawnette to Diana and had tried to give her his love and attention as she healed from the wounds she had received on the mountain.

But she knew something was missing in their relationship and she knew she couldn't compete with a memory or a ghost. Thomas understood these things and felt sad for her that he could not give her what she needed from him, but he did not miss her as he had thought he would.

In his dreams, he was always with Shawnette, laughing, making love, and happy. Her beautiful bright smile gave him hope every night. When he awoke he missed the dreams and stoically faced each dawn as something he had to endure.

He rarely smiled anymore, but he did find himself at Pea and Trey's more often than not. He did not plan on driving there, but he would suddenly find himself pulling his truck up the drive to their house.

They greeted him as family, with love and concern. He sometimes just quietly sat with them, never really knowing whom he was anymore or what his place in life was. What had happened on that mountain ridge had changed him forever and no matter how much he tried to forget it, he could not. He could close his eyes and still see and even smell Shawnette as she stood over him and said, "Not yet."

Pea's heart broke every time she saw his truck approaching the house, but she never allowed him to see it on her face. She understood why Diana had left, but she was sometimes unreasonably angry over Diana's lack of strength in staying with Thomas. Thomas, so handsome and so strong and so very, very sad. How could Diana have left him without even trying to work through the trauma, she wondered.

But Pea would walk out onto the portico and wave as Thomas's truck slowly made its way to their home. Between her sister's family and Thomas, she sometimes wondered if Trey felt that Pea had become a magnet for the lost and broken souls around them.

She had once asked Trey about it in the quiet hours of the night after the twins were down and they were alone for a few precious hours. He had smiled at her, shrugged his shoulders and kissed her forehead.

"You were always the strongest of all of us. Nobody saw it, but I did and I loved you for it. It's okay. Maybe you're the pole star who guides us all."

"Whatever," he continued. "Don't worry about it. We're all where we're meant to be."

She clasped him to her body and held him tightly that night. She didn't feel strong. She felt he was her strength. But she had finally forgiven herself and found a happiness that she could not have imagined having five years previously.

Three toddlers had changed all their lives and sometimes as the children clambered around the house, especially entranced by Thomas, Pea noticed that the few smiles and laughter Thomas had anymore for anyone or anything came from the endless attention of the children to show him their latest Lego creations and Thomas the Train engines. Even Ree's daughter would build small planes for Thomas to fly over her head as her tight curls shook with her laughter.

Perhaps the children gave him a hope for a life he had lost when Diana had left him, when Shawnette had appeared to him on that mountain, Pea thought. Since she and Thomas were the only ones to see what really happened, how Shawnette had kept him alive and how Alicia had kept Pea from killing another man, she knew that there was an unbreakable bond between them.

Except for their brief conversation, she had never discussed with anyone other than Thomas what had happened and she was almost positive that Thomas had not either.

But it did not stop her from worrying about him and at one time she had wondered if Trey felt secondary to her silent alliance with Thomas, but he never said a word if he did feel that way and he always welcomed Thomas as much of a brother as he did Joseph.

What Pea did not know was that Trey was happier than he had been since he had been a child. He now had the family he had never had by having them all there in his home, even though Thomas went home every night. Trey had been so alone as a child that Pea and her "tribe" as he sometimes called them were everything he had ever wanted.

Sometimes he watched her and his boys in amazement. How could one chance encounter in a book store with a beautiful, frightened woman have made his life so good, so right? He would smile at her across the room and she would return his smile, not knowing just how much she had changed his life or the lives of everyone around her.

Joseph did the same thing with Ree, but always with concern masked by his smile. Ree had changed after the mountain, even though she had not been there. Joseph thought that her capture by Manley and his own heart attack, and the events on the ridge had made her afraid to the point that he was seriously considering talking to her about seeing a therapist. Each day, she withdrew even further from the world. Now she would rarely leave the farm to go grocery shopping. She had discovered online shopping and had begun using their free delivery services for everything from diapers to pasta.

He had decided that he was going to talk to Pea and Trey about getting her out. He had been asked to speak at a behavioral profiling conference at the University of Central Florida in Orlando and he knew that if he did not get her away from the farm that he might never get her to leave. His family had come to Staunton after the birth of their daughter and had found a much changed woman in Mary.

Both his parents were concerned with the traumas she had endured and her inability to cope with what had happened and her growing fear of the outside world. That they would voice these concerns made him realize that she was in trouble. They had never been overtly happy about his marriage or his living in Staunton so their concern forced him to face what he wanted to ignore.

Whatever worries they had had about the marriage had disappeared with that visit. Their new granddaughter brought a bond to all of them that he had never felt with anyone other than Mary or his grandmother.

He decided after their visit that he could not let her fears cripple her further. He had to help her escape her self-imposed imprisonment somehow, someway.

So, as Pea sat blowing bubbles for her sons and her niece, her sister and Joseph were at the airport with Trey, preparing to fly to Orlando.

None of them realized that the two were about to fly into the worst nightmare they had ever experienced, one that made everything that had come before a simple prelude to the open door to hell.

Ree, Pea's beautiful, angelic and gentle, auburn haired sister was about to be mistaken for an angel by a man who thought his killings were done in the service of God.

Had Pea even suspected this, she would never have allowed Ree to leave the farm and probably would have never left there herself. But as the old saying went, "Man plans and God laughs." Pea just never dreamed it could happen to any of them again.

Chapter Three

Trey helped his sister-in-law and Joseph unload their luggage from his car and carry it into the Shenandoah Valley Regional Airport. He noticed that Mary's hands were trembling a little as she tried to lift her carry-on bag from the trunk. Joseph was so preoccupied with tickets, gathering their papers together, and getting their baggage checked that he did not see Mary's hands shaking.

Trey put his arm around her waist and guided her towards her husband.

"Don't be afraid. You two need this and you know your daughter is safe with us. I promise," he whispered in her ear as they entered the terminal.

She honestly tried to smile and joke away her jitters.

"Oh, it's just small planes. Small planes and rock stars," she replied.

Trey laughed and hugged her waist tighter.

"Then you have absolutely nothing to worry about as you're not a rock star. That weird music gene all went to your sister."

"Which probably explains her fear of flying," Mary smiled shakily and stood back from Trey just as Joseph approached them.

"We're all ready," he said. He appeared more flustered than Mary, his face flushed and his eyes glancing over at the small TSA gate. He was almost angry with the entire procedure of checking in and he had complained about it all the way from the farm to the airport. Trey knew that Joseph was more concerned with his wife than the TSA, but he had just nodded in agreement with Joseph. No use borrowing trouble, he thought.

"Trey, thanks for everything," Joseph reached out to shake Trey's hand and Mary leaned in to hug him.

"You have all the numbers. Call us no matter what the time is if you need to. I hate leaving you and Pea with three toddlers. Maybe . . ."

"Stop worrying. Get some sun while he sits in seminars at the university and listens to bureaucrats all day. Read. Relax. Shop," Trey said interrupting her.

"And, you can do this for us this fall. Pea wants to go to Manhattan after the last harvest. I think she has some concerts on her agenda, so don't think this is a freebie," he added.

That made both Mary and Joseph laugh.

"Yeah, Pea on a plane. Now that does make me smile," Mary said and waved as she and Joseph headed through the TSA check-in.

Trey watched them through the small glassed-in terminal until they boarded the plane bound for Orlando.

As he drove back to the farm, he thought that he should call them and have them ship some fresh Florida oranges and Key Limes back to the farm. He wanted to make a fresh Key Lime pie with real Key Limes for Pea and her tribe.

He thought about how Pea had changed. He wondered if she had really changed or had she just escaped from her own fears the way Mary needed to do so now. Pea was 35, the same age his mother had been when his mother had died. He thought of the boys growing up without a mother and a chill passed up his spine. He could not let that happen. His children could not grow up lonely and forgotten the way he had.

As he pulled up to the house, he watched as Pea and the children played in a cloud of bubbles that she was creating by spinning the soap wand in circles. The children were running around her, each trying to catch the bubbles.

She finally dropped to the ground and the three toddlers piled on her, each of them trying to pull her back to her feet. She heard Trey shut the car door just a second before the children did.

The boys ran to him, each grabbing a leg and trying to climb up into his arms. But Taylor stayed back, standing next to where Pea sat on the ground. Her eyes were beginning to well up with tears and Pea saw the fear before she could open her mouth to cry. She reached over to Taylor and took her in her arms and hugged her tightly.

"Mommy," the little girl cried out and Trey and the boys froze where they stood. No matter how much Mary and Joseph had tried to prepare her for their absence, no two year old could really understand, especially when she had never spent one night away from her parents.

Pea looked to Trey, unsure of how to handle this. She felt a bit stupid for not expecting the child's tears at her parents' sudden disappearance. Trey sat both the boys down next to Pea and then sat himself on the ground next to all of them.

"Taylor, you know about airplanes. Well, your Mommy and Daddy got on an airplane to go get some fresh orange juice. They're going all the way to the magical kingdom of sunshine where oranges taste sweeter than anywhere in the world and they're going to bring the oranges back just for you," he said.

Taylor and the boys stared at Trey as he told them a fairy tale about the magical kingdom in a place called Florida where you could pick the fruit off the trees and drink the juice from the fruit instead of from bottles.

Pea leaned back in the grass and watched her family as Trey wove his tale of enchantment of a land where the ocean lived and it was always sunny and warm. He was a better father than he would ever know and it made her love him more than she thought she possibly could. He and their children were the answers to her prayers.

She thought of Alicia and how Manley had ignored her, how he had taken Alicia's life for spite and greed, and Pea's face clouded over. She looked away from her family and out towards the fields of summer hay. It wasn't fair that Alicia had never had this love from a good father.

She jumped up and walked up the steps to the portico so that Trey and the children could not see her tears. One day she would take the boys to their sister's grave, but not now. Not for a long time.

While she was lost in her thoughts of Alicia, she didn't notice that Trey had gathered the children together and had handed their care over to Mrs. Franklin. Trey walked back to the portico where she stood and draped his arm over his wife's shoulder.

"Alicia?"

She wiped her eyes with the back of her hand and just nodded. He pulled her to him and let her rest her head against his chest.

"Sometimes, when I see you with the boys, I think of her. I can't help it. She deserved you, too. A father who loved her and didn't, didn't . . ."

He brushed his hand against her blonde hair and leaned down to kiss the top of her head. What could he say that would ease her pain, he wondered. Nothing. Not one thing. He couldn't imagine her grief, especially after their boys had arrived. Losing them was impossible for him to even consider.

"I'm sorry," she said and stepped away from him, trying to pull herself together.

"I feel both lost and found, guilty, I suppose."

She shook her head and walked over to the steps.

"It's just that it's that time of the year. I can't help thinking of her. I miss her still. Over five years and I think of what she would look like now. She would be almost twelve and she would have loved her brothers."

"I should have done more to protect her. I should have . . ."

Trey moved behind her and wrapped his arms around her, trying to ease her pain.

"Pea, stop it now. You were a good mother to her. He took her from you. You couldn't have known," Trey said.

"But . . ."

"No," Trey said. "You were and are a good mother. It's unthinkable to me now that we have the boys what you go through each day, missing her and seeing her in the kids, but you cannot blame yourself."

He took her hand and led her towards the front door. He lifted her hand and kissed it before they entered the house.

"Come. Mrs. Franklin probably has managed to get their lunches. Let's go join our family," he said and smiled.

Oh god, Pea thought. How I love this man.

Somewhere over the Carolinas on the airplane, Joseph began to lose the feeling in his right hand. Mary squeezed it as the small plane hit a little more turbulence than he had expected during the flight.

He looked over at her and saw that her face was white with fear. It made her hair look even more fiery, her blue eyes brighter than normal. For a brief moment, he thought of the Dante Rossetti painting of Rossetti's wife, Beatrice. Such beauty and such deep sadness.

"Mary, dear, I'm losing the feeling in my hand," he said.

She turned to him as if he were a stranger and then looked down at their clasped hands.

"Oh god, Joseph, I'm sorry. I didn't realize I was holding it so tight."

He kissed her cheek and pushed her auburn curls away from her face.

"She's ok. I bet they're eating lunch now or getting ready for their afternoon nap. We'll call the minute we land. I promise. She's going to be fine."

"You promise?" Mary asked just as she had asked Trey.

"I miss her. I feel as if someone has pulled my heart out."

Joseph placed his hand over her heart, her thin silk blouse the only separation between his hand and her breast.

"It's still there, beating for all three of us. I promise it will be okay."

She lay her head on his shoulder and sighed. She knew he was right. They needed this time together and their daughter would be fine. But being rational still didn't change how much she missed her baby.

She closed her eyes and tried not to think of anything. She took Joseph's hand again and loosely laced her fingers with his.

"I won't squeeze too hard this time. I'm going to try and sleep. Wake me when we get ready to land."

He kissed her cheek again and leaned his head back and closed his eyes as well. He had gotten her this far. Everything would be okay. He knew it would be.

Chapter Four

Raymond Templeton was pushing a cleaning cart through the large lobby of the Criminal Justice building at the University of Central Florida as Joseph strode through the front doors and stopped to look for someone involved with his and Mary's arrangements for the duration of the conference. Raymond was bored and wanted to be home where three angels awaited him. Joseph's appearance in an expensive suit and his haste into the building irritated Raymond. Another self important and ignorant mortal, thought Raymond.

Raymond despised the teachers and the students and the staff equally. If he were not forced to present this façade by circumstance, he would walk away from them and their false idols called science and technology. But, in order to maintain God's mission, he knew that he had to live among them in order to attain money.

As Joseph was probably just someone there for the conference, Raymond ignored him and was just about to leave the lobby when he spied Mary entering the building.

For a brief moment, he almost forgot to breathe. She was stunning. The sun illuminating her brilliant halo of red hair and the glow of her golden wings made him almost dizzy. In the five years he had worked here, not one angel had ever walked through those doors until today. Her beauty was transcendent. He saw her transparent wings stretch as she waved and smiled at the man in the expensive suit who had entered the building ahead of her.

Oh good God, he thought. Thank you, Lord. God had sent him one of his better angels as a reward for Raymond's hard work in freeing the angels from their mortal chains. Raymond remembered to breathe and suddenly thought that he had much work to do to prepare for her tests and ascendancy, but right now, in the lobby of the Justice building, this moment would remain frozen in his memory forever. He believed that God had truly blessed him. She had to be an angel. No mortal woman could be so flawless.

Neither Joseph nor Mary noticed the tall man in the corner of the lobby with the cleaning cart. They were trying to get registered, find out about their accommodations, and make sure that any emergency calls or messages would be routed to them immediately no matter where they might be. They were also dressed for the conference in clothing that, while professional, was too warm for Florida in the summer. Neither of them had really had any idea just how hot Orlando would be.

Mary, who had dressed in a pale ivory linen suit, took deep breaths of the cold air in the lobby and wished now that she had pinned her heavy hair up. Just a few minutes in the heat had left her weak.

She smiled at the young woman with the name badge that said "Teri" as the woman confirmed Joseph as their featured speaker and was calling someone to alert the people in charge of the conference that he had arrived.

Mary wished that the woman would hurry up so they could get the formalities done so she could call home and get out of this suit. She wondered what had possessed her to wear stockings. She looked around the lobby for a quiet place to call and check in with Pea.

The lobby was starting to fill with summer school students leaving class for the day and the only remote place was occupied by a janitor who was staring at them. She smiled nervously at him and turned to take Joseph's arm.

Raymond felt actual pain when she smiled at him. His heart hurt and he knew he would not be denied this angel. God was good. Praise him, he thought as he continued to watch the angel's transparent wings fold around the man in the suit.

Raymond did not like that. Why was she protecting the man?

Mary noticed that Joseph seemed very pleased to be there and greeted his hosts warmly, yet never failed to introduce her to each of them. She still felt out of place and thought of her daughter's smile in an attempt to steady her nerves. She masked her stress and shook hands with the people gathering around her husband.

She knew Joseph's reputation and how he could talk so easily with anyone. She smiled again and stepped back a bit to allow him room to speak with the people around them. Most of them ignored her after their initial introduction and focused on Joseph. She felt her chest tighten as more people gathered around them, some of them almost pushing her away from Joseph. At one point, she lost hold of his hand and was almost shoved away from the table.

She looked for some refuge to escape the crowd. She knew the panic she felt in her chest was coming from within her own mind, but it did not help. She took deep breaths and waited patiently to the side. She knew then that she would not be spending much time at this conference. She thought that perhaps she might find more peace at the house they were staying. Perhaps she could even go running in the evening. Maybe there was a park nearby.

Raymond listened carefully as everything took place. Mr. & Mrs. Joseph Hallett. When he heard Joseph mention the conference, he dismissed it as he could not take his eyes off the angel standing next to Hallett and how she was being pushed away from the man. Raymond watched as her wings were pushed farther away from him, until they folded against her back as she bowed her head and stood away. He believed that she was praying and he bowed his head and briefly spoke to the Lord as well.

Joseph noticed that Mary had been shunted away from him and he gently pushed through the people around him to reach her. Trained for years in spotting behavioral tics and things that were out of place, Joseph noticed the tall man's almost obsessive stare directed at Mary. He knew his wife was a beautiful woman, but this man seemed wrong, one of those out of place things, no matter that the man looked to be an employee of the university.

Joseph placed his hand on Mary's arm and stared back at the man, who suddenly moved the cleaning cart away and smiled as he passed away from them further into the building. The man set off alarms in his head that he ignored and would later regret that act.

Joseph turned to his hosts and asked for directions to where they would be staying. Young Teri informed them that they would be staying at one of the professors' homes in Bartram, giving him directions, information about the area, and a set of keys to the house. The professor and his wife were in Italy. He had taken his sabbatical to do research on Italian police and Interpol techniques for a book he was doing on terrorist cells in Italy.

"You'll love Professor Teel's home. Close to school, shops and Cady Way Park. Oh, and I forgot to mention that he and his wife have a spectacular garden and pool," Teri said.

"Well, I believe we're going to get some rest before this evening. So if you'll excuse us, we'll see everyone this evening," he said and smiled broadly.

He turned away from them and whispered into his wife's ear.

"Mary," Joseph said quietly. "Let's go. I think we should find someplace less crowded."

While he sensed her unease in the crowd, he also did not want to alarm her about the man with the cleaning cart whose attention to Mary worried him. He looked around for the man, but now did not see him anywhere. He shook his head and wondered if the last few years were starting to catch up with him.

What was the old saying? He wasn't being paranoid. He was just being exceptionally aware. Maybe too much, he thought.

Mary was confused by his sudden need to depart, but was relieved to get out of there. She had been oblivious to the man's attention. The conference was here. Why did Joseph want to leave? She just wanted to let him enjoy himself and find a quiet place to call their daughter. She started to feel guilty about his leaving.

I should be stronger, she thought. She took his hand in hers and wondered what had happened to the woman who had dared to flaunt their affair in the face of the dean of her law school. Her shoulders drooped. She believed that Joseph deserved someone better than her.

"Thank you for all your help, Teri," Joseph said as they left. He grasped Mary's arm, and led her to the front door of the lobby.

Raymond, who had managed to hide his rather tall form in an alcove off the lobby heard Joseph's name and then heard Joseph call the angel Mary, which Joseph would regret later. He would castigate himself for not calling her Ree as he had for the past year. But for now, Raymond saw their names as another sign from God. He was so surprised that he could not move.

Joseph and Mary. Seeking their lodgings. Could she be more than just an angel? Could it be? Could God be giving her to him as his final reward so that he, too, could ascend to heaven with her? Could the time be upon him? His mind exploded with the possibilities of the chance he might be about to be offered by God. Could their mutual ascendancy have a deeper meaning from the Revelations of John?

He knew then that there was much he had to do had to find out everything he could about them. This Mary could be the ultimate blessing God would bestow on him. Maybe she could finally release him from his own mortal shell and the poisons that filled him from his contact with mortal women.

He left the alcove and walked quickly after them, watching them as they left. He wanted to stop them and speak to them. He felt the urgent need to hear her voice, but he knew it would be most unwise to approach them. The man named Joseph was someone involved in the Justice department and God may have plans for the man. Raymond believed that he simply couldn't take the chance.

He was devastated by their departure. What if he lost her? What if he couldn't find the information he needed? He had had Mary, the holiest of women, right there in front of him and the man had taken her away. Then he thought of Mary and Joseph in the New Testament. Joseph was never really her husband. Mary's real husband was the Lord. Joseph was merely her mortal caretaker. Raymond walked away from them reluctantly. He knew it was the right thing to do. Joseph might see the glow of the Lord on

Raymond and it might frighten him enough to take Mary away forever.

As Raymond headed back to his supply closet, he became angry. The mortal had no right to usurp God's plan. How dare he take Mary from Raymond? Raymond believed that he was God's anointed and would brook no interference in the Lord's plan.

Raymond's face reddened with anger and he rushed back to the small room and began to plan. He would find everything he could about the couple. He would find out where they were staying. He would have his Mary and that mortal was a test the Lord had given him to see if Raymond were worthy of Mary, his great blessing.

He pulled out a notebook and began to write everything he knew so far and what plans he needed to make, everything he needed to do, including further research and he knew he had precious little time to do these things. The conference was only one week. One week must be a test God was giving him to procure this angel. He would find them, wherever they would be staying in Orlando and he would have his angel.

He had a small laptop set up in the back of his small room and began by trying to find anything about her or her husband on the internet. It was not a difficult task. It seemed that both of them were quite well known.

As he read of the events of the past few years that she had endured, her husband's reputation, the names of the others involved, including the other protector named Thomas, he saw all of it as a divination from God of what he had to do. That she had twice been tested by evil men and survived only strengthened his belief that she was above all the angels he had taken, including the ones he had released to heaven.

Teri, the woman from the registration desk, knocked at his door and stuck her head in the room to remind him that he would need to make sure the table linens would be delivered to the banquet hall for the dinner that evening. He stood to follow her to perform his duties. He did it quickly and tersely. He had too many things to think about to worry about these trivialities. He gathered the linens in his arms and was preparing to take them to the hall when he decided not to go there.

He realized that Teri had the information he needed and went over to her as she sat at the table, pasting a smile on his face in order to try to befriend her. If that didn't work, he would create some crisis that she would have to handle. Either way, he was going to find out where Mary would be staying.

Teri ignored his presence and continued to speak with the visitors about what he thought were inconsequential matters. He grew impatient, but waited, although she never seemed to see him. After five minutes, he gave up and stepped back from the table. He had discovered nothing and felt more frustrated. He would watch the table and when Teri left it, he would look through the papers there.

It did not take long. After he moved away, she grabbed a sheet of paper and called to one of conference attendees leaving, running across the lobby to them.

Raymond carefully moved to the table and saw the file with Joseph Hallett's name on it and slid the file into the stack of tablecloths he had been holding. He walked away toward the banquet hall and had entered it just as Teri returned to the table.

Teri had actually been aware that Raymond was standing behind her and had purposefully ignored him. As she saw him walking into the hall, she sighed with relief. He did not annoy her. He terrified her. He reminded her of the mortician in that movie that had frightened her as a child. What was the name of it? She was preparing to go home to change for the opening banquet when she remembered. *Phantasm*. He looked just like the creepy mortician in *Phantasm*. Tall, skinny, with thinning hair and sallow skin. She shivered thinking of it.

When she arrived home having completed her registration tasks for the afternoon, she locked herself into her house and checked every window and door. She suddenly felt the need to be ill tonight, but knew she had to be there for the opening of the conference. The thought of seeing Raymond Templeton again made her feel ill. It was not a pleasant thought that she had no choice in it.

Chapter Five

Pea had just gotten the children down for their naps when she felt her iPhone vibrate in her jeans pocket. She answered it as she slipped down the staircase so as not to waken the sleeping toddlers. She was exhausted and realized how much she had come to depend on Ree's presence in the house.

"They're all three sleeping soundly," she whispered as she reached the bottom of the stairs. For some reason, she suddenly thought of her great danes lying in a heap there and a chill touched the nape of her neck. She pulled the band from her hair, and rubbed her neck as her sister spoke to her from Florida.

"Did she cry when we didn't return? She's never been alone and I've worried that she might have been scared," Ree said to her sister.

Pea flopped onto the couch that Ree had proven correct in her prediction that she would regret having bought. When she had been nine months pregnant with the twins, she had had to have Trey pull her up every time she sat on it. But, now that she was back to her old weight, she sank into the softness of the cushions to ease her tired back.

"Alone? What are we? Aliens? She's fine. Yes, there was a moment or two of tears, but Trey told the three children about the magical trip you and Joseph had taken. You would have loved it. He turned your trip to Florida into a fairy tale and after that she was fine."

Pea could hear the catch in her sister's breathing and wanted Ree to know her daughter was safe. In Florida, Mary looked out the passenger window of the rental car and raised her hand to her cheek to block a tear threatening to fall from behind her sunglasses. She didn't want Joseph to see her upset. She already felt guilty about their leaving the conference registration so soon.

Instead, Mary smiled and laughed and told her sister that the trip was wonderful, that everyone had been so kind, that Orlando was beautiful, and that they were having a great time. She lied.

And Pea could hear the lie in every word her sister spoke. She sat up on the sofa and looked out the window to the early hay bowing down in the wind, the color changing from a matte green to shimmering blades in the sunlight.

"Ree, Taylor is really okay, but I'm worried about you. I assume you're with Joseph right now. Can you call me later when you're alone?"

Her sister paused and was silent.

"Ree, talk to me or I'm getting on a plane. You're scaring me."

"Okay, I can do that," Mary said. "Well, we're here at the house the university has let us use while we're here so I have to go. I'll call tonight about all the stuff going on. Kiss Taylor for me. Gotta go."

Pea held the iPhone in front of her and stared at it. What the hell? Maybe she had been wrong to let Joseph talk her into helping him convince Ree to go with him. Pea looked up at the ceiling and listened carefully to see if she heard the children. The house was quiet except for the sound of running water in the kitchen.

She walked to the kitchen and found Mrs. Franklin rinsing half runner beans for supper.

"Mrs. Franklin, I need to walk down to the barn. Could you listen for the kids? They should sleep for another hour or so, but just in case."

Mrs. Franklin laughed and nodded her head toward the baby monitors on top of the Hoosier cabinet.

"I haven't heard a peep from them since you took them up, except for the boys whispering before they fell asleep. If I hear them, I'll go upstairs."

Pea smiled and said thank you. She went out the back screen door and held it so that it closed quietly. It was so humid today. Halfway to the barn, she thought that she should have brought Trey something to drink. He was probably burning up in this heat.

Just as she arrived at the open barn doors, she saw her husband sit down on the stairs to the loft and wipe his forehead, his dark curls damp with sweat. She walked over to him and sat next to him. He leaned over to kiss her and she leaned away from him.

"Eww. You smell like the cows," she said and laughed.

He laughed with her and grabbed her by the waist, pulling her tightly to his chest and nuzzled her neck. She feinted small blows against his back, but ultimately embraced him and kissed him hard.

"Don't make me take you up into the loft. I'll make you forget what I smell like," he said.

She jumped up and ran to the loft, knowing that he would follow her. They had never "christened" the barn, although they had done so in almost every room in the house. As he reached her across the floor of the loft, she could feel a breeze through the open loft doors.

"Wait, where's Mr. Franklin?" she asked as he began unzipping her jeans.

"Gone into Staunton. Won't be back till the end of the day. Now, where was I?" he said as he slid her loose jeans from her hips and then slipped her t-shirt over her head.

She unzipped his pants and pressed into him as she kissed him. It took less than a minute for them to remove the rest of their clothes. They were so involved in their love play that they failed to notice that the rough boards of the loft was their only bed.

Trey stopped and looked down at the floor with the detritus of decades littering it.

"This won't do," he said and stepped away. He went to a shelf and found an old coverlet that had probably been there as long as the barn had been there and laid it upon the floor.

They sank to the covered floor and he began to nibble at her breasts as he worked his way down her belly. By the time he reached her inner thighs, he was lifting her buttocks upward to reach his target. She inhaled sharply and grasped his dark curls as he brought her closer to climax.

Just as suddenly, he stopped and moved upward and lifted her body up and she sat with her open legs wrapped around his waist, guiding him into her.

Neither of them was aware of the heat or their surroundings as they finished their lovemaking. It was only afterwards, as a warm breeze flit across their bodies that were covered in a sheen of sweat that Pea lay her head in the crook of Trey's elbow. She traced a line in the shiny dampness of his chest and looked up to him and smiled.

"So, the blanket's here from past excursions?" she asked.

He rolled on his side to face her and rolled one of her pink nipples between his thumb and index finger.

"Never. This thing's been here as long as I can remember. You are my first here."

He leaned over and gently kissed the nipple he had been caressing.

"Oh, you're starting something again," she whispered.

Just as she rose to meet his kiss, she heard a voice call their names.

Damn, she thought. Who is that, she thought, then recognized the deep voice of Thomas.

Trey looked over to the stairs and then to her. She had to stifle a giggle.

"Thomas, uh, give me a minute," Trey called out and quickly pulled his jeans and shirt on. He was about to head to the stairs when Pea hissed at him and pointed at his bare feet. He slid his sockless feet into his work boots and had almost finished buttoning his shirt as he reached the top of the stairs. He looked over to see Pea's blonde hair and nude body glowing in the late afternoon sunlight. She looked like a Wyeth painting.

"You owe me," she mouthed to him and he smiled as he headed down to greet Thomas and get him back to the house so Pea could dress.

Pea lay in the light of the open loft and stretched her body out like a satisfied cat. After a few minutes of peace, she thought that she could almost sleep there, but instead she finally rose and dressed, folded the blanket and put it back on the shelf. She smiled as she thought of future opportunities it might provide. She was about to head downstairs when she saw Trey's boxers and socks on the floor. She rolled them up and put them with the coverlet. She'd return later the retrieve all of them for the wash when the Franklins and Thomas were gone.

As she walked alone back to the house, she thought of Ree and wished she had thought to talk to Trey about Ree before their little loft adventure. She knew the children would be waking soon and wanted to make sure that Taylor wasn't upset by Ree and Joseph's absence when she awoke.

She sighed and wondered if Florida could possibly be as humid as the Shenandoah Valley was in the summer. She had never been to Florida, but she thought it couldn't be any worse than Louisiana had been when she had visited there with Manley. Damn. Would his name ever leave her? She shook her body as if to shuck off the taint of his existence from her past. Alicia. As long as Alicia was in her heart, she would be cursed by what he had done to her and how she had avenged herself. Damn him, she thought. She hoped he burned in hell for what he had done.

Sometimes she longed for the less humid climes of the Greenbrier Valley. She and Ree really should go there more often, especially her. She thought of the small cemetery and suddenly felt a sharp pang of homesickness.

How can I feel both places are home? She wondered if they should spend some time at the Greenbrier place. She really missed it today. No, she thought, she missed Alicia. That's why she was thinking of Greenbrier County this afternoon.

Better to think of the afternoon she had just spent with Trey and their children. Get Manley's poison from her veins. As she reached the back door she could hear Trey and Thomas laughing in the kitchen, teasing Mrs. Franklin about needing to make more beans.

She was about to shoo them from the kitchen when she heard the voices of her sons talking with her niece on one of the baby monitors.

"Could you two grab the kids so Mrs. Franklin and I can finish getting supper?"

Thomas gave her a smug grin and then nodded his head in her direction.

Pea felt her cheeks burning. He knew what they had been doing in the loft. Trey saw her embarrassment and tried to allay her unease with a joke.

"You mean Mrs. Franklin will be cooking and you'll be watching. Come on, Thomas. I need to clean up before supper anyway and before my wife throws something at me," he said and went towards the door from the kitchen into the main house.

Pea heard her niece's teary voice on the monitor and forgot about literally getting caught with her pants down. She followed the men from the kitchen and went to help with the children. She sighed as she realized that this was going to be a long week.

She had no idea that the week would turn into the longest and possibly worst month in her life.

Chapter Six

Mary followed Joseph into the house and was surprised by the post modern furnishings. She hadn't really known what she had expected, maybe something more academic or more tropically inspired, but the house was a beautiful example of mid twentieth century interior design.

But best of all, it was cool and dry. She walked over to a bank of glass walls at the opposite side of the large open room and saw a gorgeous tropical pool with a small waterfall and nature themed design. It looked as cool as the house felt, but she knew it was probably close to 90 degrees out there.

"God, I'm so tired," Joseph said as he walked up behind her and looked out at the back yard.

She turned to face him and smiled. He was doing this for her. She knew he wasn't tired. In fact, she was fairly certain that he wanted to get back to the university as soon as possible. She kissed him and laid her hand upon his cheek.

"Joseph, love, you are not tired. Don't pretend to be for me. I know you want to get back to the conference."

He started to protest, but his words were stopped by her kiss.

"Go on back for a while. I'm going to take a short nap and then get acclimated to this house. I may even take a swim when the sun goes down. But you have work to do and I'm just in the way."

He sighed and walked away to the front door and slammed it as he exited without a word to her. She sat down on the vinyl sofa. She was a little shocked. She had expected him to at least try and convince her to go with him. That he would just leave . . . she was not prepared for that.

She felt tears forming in her eyes and she grew angry with him. He could have at least said something, anything, to change her mind, she thought. Just as she was rising to go in search of a bedroom, Joseph returned into the house with their suitcases. She continued to walk away from him. If he wasn't going to talk to her, he'd regret bringing her on his trip.

"Ree, stop. Where do you want me to put these?"

She stopped and glared at him. She wanted to tell him to put them where the sun didn't shine, but she refrained from cursing at him and pointed to the bedroom she was standing near.

He sighed again and dragged the cases through the house. Damn. What the hell was wrong with her? He felt as if everything he said or did was wrong. After getting the luggage in the bedroom, he went to find her in the kitchen where she was pouring herself a glass of wine.

"Mary! What the hell is going on? Why are you angry? What have I done to deserve the silent treatment because I thought you were having a good time?"

She drained the glass of merlot and began to pour more into her glass. She stared at him.

"A good time, watching pretty coeds fawning all over you while I get pushed aside? You're the man of the hour. I'm just another piece of luggage. You could have at least pretended to want me to go tonight."

He looked at her in amazement and then began to laugh. He went around the kitchen island and pulled a glass down to pour some of the merlot for himself.

"Fine. Just fine. Laugh," she said.

Oh, he knew what fine meant in her native dialect. It meant she was royally pissed. He leaned over and kissed her cheek before she could move away from him.

"Mary, my love, those coeds aren't even close to your beauty and may I remind you that they're mostly your age. I wanted you here with me because I love you, even when you're irrationally tired."

Mary stepped backward.

"Irrational? I'm being paranoid, is that what you're saying?"

He saw that this was not going to be an argument he had a chance in hell of winning.

"Okay. Here's what I'm going to do. I'm going to cancel everything, stay here with you tonight and then we can go home tomorrow. How's that?"

Mary blushed and looked away from him in embarrassment. She twirled the merlot in the glass and had trouble finding the right words. What was wrong with her?

"No, Joseph, no. Shit. I don't know what's wrong with me. I can't explain these insecurities I'm feeling. I just felt so useless today and I missed Taylor so much. I'm sorry."

He brought her close to him and let her lay her head on his shoulder.

"I love you and our daughter more than anything. This conference seemed like a chance for us to have some time alone, but I'd rather have the two of you than anything I might get from this conference."

Mary wiped the tears away and lifted her head and tried to shake off the feeling of dread she had.

"No, you're right. I'm being melodramatic. Let's go to the dinner tonight. We both do need this break."

"Well, come on. We have time to rest a little before we have to get ready for this evening," he said as he led her to the bedroom.

As they reached the bedroom door he stopped and reached over and gently touched the pale skin of her face.

"Mary, don't ever think that you're not beautiful. You're everything I've ever wanted. Not one of those girls can compare to you," he said with a smile.

She returned his smile and began to undress slowly.

"Show me," she said. "Show me now."

Outside the house, hidden in the lush greenery around the pool, their movements were watched by Raymond Templeton. As he saw his Mary removing her clothing, the man called Joseph walked over and closed the vertical blinds.

Raymond knew what was about to happen and he was furious to the point of rushing into the house, killing the man and taking his Mary right then. He saw that this Joseph was not a safe man for her.

The one thing that stopped him was the sight of her nude body, her magnificent wings spread high and lit with the golden feathers that were transparent to everyone but him. He saw that she was enslaved by mortal obligations to this man as Mary had been to her Joseph in the Bible.

He crept into the house through the front door that Joseph had forgotten to lock. He could hear them in the bedroom but not see them as Joseph had closed the door.

What could he do? He listened to them as they made the sounds mortals made as they fornicated. He held his hands to his ears and began to rock back and forth in the corner where he squatted to hide.

Why was God punishing him by making him witness to Mary's shame? Then he realized that it was not Mary's shame he was being forced to witness. Mary was Joseph's wife and God wanted him to know that there were some things Raymond should not do, especially interfere when Joseph was there. But when Joseph was not with her, Mary would be Raymond's and he now understood God's message.

Joseph could not take her to the ecstasy of God's light, but Raymond could and it was his job to do it. He slipped from the house and drove to his house in Christmas. He would have to pray much tonight and he would have to consult his angels.

Mary was more than one of his angels. Mary was the holiest of all. He had to ask God to show him the way. His shame at what he had had to hear was God telling him something. Now he had to go home and decipher what God was telling him to do.

When he arrived at his home, he went to the cabin where his three angels waited. He took the one who was to begin the strappado test tonight. He lay her down, attached the leather harness to her, and used the pulley to lift her up. He knelt before her and began to recite the Revelation of

John. When he looked up, he saw that she was writhing in pain from her arms being pulled upward and away from her shoulders.

When he saw the movement of her naked body and the feeble attempts of her small wings to lift her, he did something he had never done before. He lowered her body just far enough that he could insert his instrument into her while standing. He grabbed her hips and pulled her hard down on himself which pulled the strappado even tighter against her shoulders. Had she not been gagged, she would have been screaming. As it was, the pain and writhing of her body made the pounding of her hips against his body more than he could bear.

With each thrust he began to say the Lord's Prayer. He grew more excited until he did something that had also never happened – he began to speak in tongues, what he had never been able to achieve, what he believed was the language of the angels. By the time he felt the poisons pour into her, she had fainted from the pain and her wings had grown even smaller. He felt exultant at his achievement and took one of her breasts in his teeth and began to tear at it, chewing it open until her blood covered both of them.

He lowered her to the ground and removed the strappado. As he carried her to her small cell and laid her on her cot, he stopped and looked to the other angels. They closed their eyes and dared not look at him. He left the angel he had ravaged on the cot and walked nude down the path back to his house.

He now knew that he had not been taking his tests far enough. The release of the poison from his member had felt so good that he now saw it as a sign from God that this was what he would have to do with the three angels before he could ascend with Mary. His clarity of mind had never been stronger and he had never felt more sure of his path.

Darkness had fallen as he reached the house. He paused by the pool and looked up to the heavenly firmament and fell to his knees as a shooting star burned quickly across the sky. Praise God. He began to weep as his blood streaked body shone in the starlight.

He was right. He now knew his path. He would take his Mary tonight and they would rise to heaven together after the other angels ascended. God willed it. The meteor was God's word to him that the last days were finally here.

Chapter Seven

While Pea and her extended family dined on fresh half runners, new potatoes, and crisp fried chicken, a luxury they had only when Joseph was away as his diet restrictions forbade the traditional southern meal, while Raymond Templeton began his drive to the university after receiving his latest revelation, Mary and Joseph were entering the banquet hall for the opening of the conference.

Joseph kept Mary's hand firmly clasped in his as they were surrounded by the conference attendees, including students, faculty, and people Joseph knew from his work. He felt her hand being pulled away and he stopped and took her elbow to place her firmly next to him.

She had seemed so fragile when they had made love that afternoon that he had been almost afraid of hurting her. At one point he had actually stopped and rolled to his side to make sure she was okay. She had barely spoken and she had moaned softly as he moved within her.

"Are you okay? Ree, am I being too rough?" he asked as he placed his hand upon her shoulder. He had stared at her face and half expected tears to be falling, but he was surprised to see a smile there.

Instead of pulling him back onto her, she had moved him to his back and straddled him, guiding him into her and moving slowly up and down. He watched as her whole body glowed as she closed her eyes and leaned her head back, her long auburn hair swaying with each movement.

He became more excited and began to match her downward thrusts with his own upward thrusts. Just as she climaxed, he felt himself release himself into her and she leaned down, sliding her body prone against his as she shivered with the small tremors moving from inside her to her other muscles.

Without removing himself from her, he rolled her over and began to kiss her throat, her lips, any part of her face that he could. And that was when he tasted the salty tears he had not seen as they had come together for his eyes had closed just at the end.

He had stopped kissing her and wiped the tears from her cheeks. He had not spoken. He could not give her what she needed because he did not understand what it was she needed.. All he could do was love her and hold her and he wondered if that was enough.

He would have willingly spent the rest of the evening there in her arms, but she had slowly slid out from under him and silently walked to the bath.

She had not closed the door and he had heard the water from the shower begin. He had swung his legs to the bedside and sat with both hands supporting him as he thought about how he could fix his broken wife.

She had never really recovered from being kidnapped by Manley. Before the kidnapping, she had been so strong and defiant in the face of any obstacle. She had loved him feverishly, abandoning all thoughts but their mutual pleasure. But after Manley . . . after Manley, and after events on "The Ridge", she had hidden herself away, alternately afraid and angry without reason. Joseph had hoped the trip to Florida would help the other Mary come back, the brave one, the one who would have not let anyone hurt her or intimidate her, but so far it had not happened.

He had thought of the old Elton John song, "High Flying Bird" and wondered if she thought he would hurt her or if loving him would. She had lost weight and was not just fragile, but frail. She had never had to lose the "baby weight" as Pea had called it. While Pea worked to get back to her old shape and weight, she had watched her sister's weight vanish effortlessly. Joseph knew that afternoon as she had showered that the quick weight change had been, while not abnormal, unusual.

He had glanced toward the steam coming from the open bathroom and realized that Pea had been right. Mary would have to see someone before this situation got worse. He hoped that it was not too late, but he had been so happy with her seeming happiness with him and Taylor that he had ignored Mary's growing depression and agoraphobic tendencies.

When the sound of the shower stopped and after a few minutes, she had reentered the bedroom, her body covered from the neck down with an oversized bath sheet. That was something different, too, he had realized. The only time he had seen her nude in the last year was when they were making love. The rest of the time she was careful to cover herself in his presence.

He had reached out his right hand to her.

"Mary, come here."

She had walked slowly across the room to him, her steps tentative.

"Please," he said, raising his hand higher.

She reached him, but did not take his hand and instead had clasped the towel to her body tightly.

He had pulled her standing form between his legs and tugged the bath sheet from her. She had resisted at first and then let go and sighed.

"If you want to make love again . . ." she had started to say.

"Stop it," he had said softly. "Stop."

The sheet had lay puddled at her feet as she stood naked before him. He had not touched her, but he had looked up and seen shame and fear in her eyes and it saddened him. He knew her own insecurities and doubts had done this to her, but it had not made him hurt for her any less.

"I love you."

She had tried to smile, but the smile never reached her eyes.

"Mary, we need help," he had said, using "we" instead of "you" to keep her from feeling more guilt.

Her face had clouded over and reddened.

"Help with what? Aren't you happy? Is something wrong?"

He had stood up next to her. God, he had thought, I have trouble even thinking straight when she's standing this close to me.

"Things aren't . . . aren't the same. I love you and I believe you love me, but it's as if something's between us."

She had bent and picked up the bath sheet and wrapped it around her body again. She had looked into his eyes and he had seen a flicker of anger there for a brief second.

"Well, there certainly wasn't anything between us a few minutes ago. At least not from my perspective," she had said and walked over to her luggage and removed toiletries and clothing.

"That's not what I'm talking about. Damn it, Mary. Stop and talk to me."

He had strode across the room to her without covering himself and had placed his hands on her upper arms. She had suddenly jerked away from him and had then realized that he was nude and aroused. She had bit her lower lip and glanced away, not knowing whether to laugh or cry.

"What?" he had asked and then had looked down.

"Oh, for Christ's sake. I can't even argue with you without . . ." He had raised his arms and then dropped them and his shoulders slumped.

And for the first time in a very, very long time, she had laughed like the Mary he had fallen in love with.

"Yes, this is what you do to me. You always have. God, woman, you make me crazy!" he had said and grabbed her and kissed her hard.

After that, they had reached a quiet, but happy truce with one another and she did seem to be his Mary again until they reached the conference and everything had begun again.

Joseph was determined that she not feel afraid or ignored or abandoned during this trip and he kept her at his side. She seemed relaxed and happy until halfway through the event when a faculty member began asking about the Redemption Ridge killers. He could feel her body tense up and he watched as she began to look around the room. He was about to speak when she interrupted him and whispered that she needed to find the Ladies room.

He nodded and reluctantly let go of her hand, but tried to keep her in view even as the man in front of him prattled on about the murders and Joseph's books on profiling serial and spree killers.

By the time Mary reached the Ladies room, she was close to hyperventilating. Luckily, no one was in there and she went into an empty stall and sat, trying to catch her breath.

Could she make it through this conference for another four days, she wondered. She knew she could not. She had to convince Joseph to allow her some time on her own. She could tell him that she wanted to explore Orlando and that she really didn't want to hear the lectures that were sure to be tediously long-winded. She could then stay at the house and relax there in safety, away from all these people who just wanted to hear about the past.

Yes, she thought. I can tell him that and he won't know that I can't stand to think about the bad things. I can convince him. I can do it.

She exited the stall and stood before the large mirror and practiced a smile that seemed genuine. It was something she was doing more and more – practicing smiling. He could never know what had really happened. He had almost died over what he had known about it. He also didn't know that she wasn't afraid of him – she was afraid of losing him if he knew the truth. She had almost told him once and then she had gotten pregnant and then there was the mess on the ridge. All of it had just delayed what she needed to say at the beginning and now she didn't know if she'd ever be able to say the words, "I was raped."

Chapter Eight

Mary never returned from the Ladies room that night. Looking back, Joseph blamed himself, had told himself that he had allowed the people around him to blind him with flattery and he believed he should have trusted his initial feelings about leaving. Looking back, he thought that there were signs he should have seen that might have saved lives. But he was wrong. There was no refuge from what fate had planned for him and his family.

When Joseph realized that Mary had been gone for over thirty minutes, he began to search the room for her head of bright auburn hair. She had worn a black lace dress and he saw that half the women in the room were wearing dark cocktail dresses.

He excused himself and rapidly walked into the outer hall and over to the door of the Ladies room just as a student in yet another dark dress exited.

"Pardon me, I'm looking for my wife. Tall redhead in a black lace dress. She went into the Ladies room and . . ."

"Not in there now. It's empty," the student said.

"Aren't you Mr. Hallett, the profiler?"

Joseph pushed past her and opened the door of the Ladies room and called out.

"Mary? Ree, are you in there? Are you okay?"

No response was the empty room.

"Mr. Hallett, there's no one in there. You can go in and look. Did you check the lobby? Maybe she stepped away from the banquet for a minute," the girl said.

Joseph rushed away from her and ran out into the empty hallway. No one. He began to get increasingly frustrated.

Damn, Mary. Don't do this to me, he thought. He was angry, thinking that she might be hiding somewhere from the crowd.

He ran outside where the valets were standing, smoking and laughing. They stopped their laughter and put their cigarettes out as he approached them.

"Have you seen my wife? The woman I arrived with? She's tall. Red hair. Thin, wearing a black lace dress?"

They stopped him before he could continue.

"We remember when you arrived. She hasn't come out this way. She must still be inside or she could be in another part of the building," one of the boys said.

He returned to the hall and looked for Teri, the organizer from the afternoon. He saw her at a table set up for late registrants and pushed through the people around the table to her.

"Mr. Hallett . . ."

Joseph never let her finish. He leaned next to her ear and whispered that his wife was missing. He asked if she could be discrete and help him find Mary.

She nodded and immediately went into the crowd to help him look. After ten minutes, she met Joseph at the front of the room.

"I can't find her anywhere, Mr. Hallett. Could she have gone home? Did you try calling her cell?"

Joseph was beyond anger and frustration now and was beginning to be afraid. He dialed Mary's phone, but it went straight to voice mail.

"No answer. Teri, she would not do this. Something is wrong."

"Okay, I'll send a couple of campus cops over to the house and we can make an announcement here in the meantime. Seriously, she's probably fine. I bet she's sitting somewhere where we can't see her. Don't worry. I know she's here.

Joseph began to shake and grasped for a chair behind him. It was Lexington all over again. Oh, God, he thought, please let her be okay. He frantically looked around the room and realized that people around him were starting to stare.

He bent forward and put his head in his hands. His heart was pounding, but no pain. He took a deep breath to try to calm himself. He could not fail her as he had in Lexington.

Mary, he thought, Mary, please be okay. Please.

Joseph could vaguely hear the announcement by Teri requesting that Mary Hallett please come to the front of the banquet room. Now people were backing away from

Joseph and separating into small groups, each of them looking for Mary to walk through the crowd to where their guest of honor sat. It was as if the entire room became quiet, everyone holding their breath in anticipation of Mary's appearance.

But after a short time had passed, Joseph looked up and around and did not see his wife and he knew that she was gone, that something truly was terribly, terribly wrong.

Pea and Trey were carrying the dishes into the kitchen and loading the dishwasher when Pea's cell began to ring. The cell was still on the dining table where Thomas was amusing the children by making origami animals out of napkins. Every time he completed one, a small chorus of voices would sing out, "Do it again! Do it again!"

Pea pushed the kitchen door open and called out to ask Thomas to answer the phone for her.

"It's probably Ree for the hundredth time today," she said to Trey as she came back into the kitchen and began to rinse off the plates as Trey loaded them into the dishwasher.

"Don't be so hard on her. This is her first time away from Taylor. Wait till we go to New York this fall. You'll be calling even more, that is if you don't hide the twins in the luggage when we go," Trey said and laughed.

She snorted and said, "Ha. Ha. I measured them already. They won't fit."

They were both laughing hard when the kitchen door swung open and Thomas stood there holding the phone out to Pea.

The both stared at him. His face was ashen and his hand holding the phone out to her was perceptibly shaking.

"Thomas, are you okay?" Trey asked.

"Pea . . ." was all Thomas could say.

Pea knew few things could evoke such a reaction in Thomas and those things were always very bad. She grabbed the phone, saw Joseph's name and said "Hello." A strange woman's voice was on the other end.

Pea stared at Thomas and Trey as she listened to the woman's voice. She dropped to the floor, still holding the phone to her ear., her face becoming paler with each moment.

Trey rushed to her and knelt on the kitchen floor next to her. In the distance, he heard one of the boys cry. Before Trey could speak, Thomas was back through the door to the children.

"Let me speak to Joseph. Now." Pea had a tone in her voice he had only heard a few times and a chill went up his spine when he heard it now.

She was nodding and saying, "Yes, yes, don't worry. We'll be there as soon as possible. Yes, I understand. Yes. Until then, yes."

She pushed the end call button and looked at Trey.

"Mary. Mary's missing. They were," she shook her head for a moment as if to get the facts straight in her head without letting her emotions take over.

She became calmer than he had ever seen her and he realized that she had called her sister Mary for one of the few times since he had met her. Fear was overwhelming his senses, but he had to try to think straight for Pea's sake.

"Take it slow. Was that Joseph? What did he say."

Pea swallowed and looked up at the ceiling. He could tell she was fighting for control of herself.

"They were at the opening banquet when Mary went to the Ladies room. She never returned. They've searched everywhere. She just vanished."

Trey tried to comprehend what Pea was saying. He stood and began to pace the small space of the kitchen, shaking his head as Pea recited the information she had been given. Not again, he thought. Not again. This could not be happening to them again.

He stopped and sat in a kitchen chair. He stared across the room at his wife. She was looking at the wall as if she could see through it all the way to Florida, as if she could see or hear her sister, her lost sister. He couldn't find the words to respond to what she had just told him. It was as if the hell of the past had begun again.

"Pea, has Joseph called the police? Hell, they're at a law enforcement conference. Surely someone saw something. Is anyone doing anything? Pea? Pea!!"

She slowly turned her head to the sound of her husband's voice. He seemed to be talking but she couldn't understand him. Suddenly she heard Zach crying and she scrambled to her feet and ran towards the sound of her son's voice. She could hear Trey behind her, still saying things she didn't understand.

She found the children in the living room floor with Thomas sitting amidst them. Zach and Jacob were fighting over a toy while Taylor stood next to Thomas with her Dora the Explorer doll, telling him about Florida. Thomas sat staring at the floor in front of him as the children played around him.

"Zach, stop that now. Bedtime. Everyone upstairs. Bed. Now. Say goodnight," she said as she scooped up Taylor and held her hand out to her twins.

Trey and Thomas hugged the boys as the twins took each other's hand and went ahead of their mother.

After Pea left the room with the children, Trey continued to stand in the hall and stare into the living room at the fireplace. They had been through so much, he thought. Why this? Why? The thought crossed his mind about Mary's depression and he briefly wondered if she might have done something. He shook his head again and knew that there was no way that she would leave her daughter. She would not just disappear.

Vanished? How could a beautiful, tall redhead just vanish in a room full of people trained to observe their environment? Someone had to have seen something. Someone.

"I'm going with you."

Trey suddenly became aware of Thomas's voice and he entered the living room and sat down in the armchair next to the door.

"Yes, of course," Trey said. He began to think of the plans he needed to make. The Franklins. He had to call them now. He had to call the airport and make reservations for the next flight to Orlando. Maybe it would better to charter a jet. They had to get down there immediately.

"Yes, Thomas. I've got to make some calls. Do you need to get anything done before we leave? I want to leave as soon as possible."

Thomas stood, holding in his large hand the Dora the Explorer doll that Taylor had handed him. He was in agony. It was as if Shawnette had disappeared all over again. This could not be fucking happening, he thought, as he lay Taylor's doll on the love seat behind him.

As he opened the front door to leave, he turned back to Trey.

"God help us all if something has happened. Pea will become an avenging angel. She'll never give this up. You know that, don't you Trey?"

Trey did not look at Thomas. He rested his head against the chair back and closed his eyes. Avenging angel, he thought. He knew exactly what Thomas was trying to say — that his wife would kill for her sister. He could feel the wetness forming in his eyes as he heard the door close. He knew one thing for certain. He would not lose his family again. Never again.

He jumped up from the chair to start making phone calls and listened as he could hear his wife pulling luggage from the hall closet. Never again. Never.

Not one of them realized that shock was coursing through their systems. They thought that after Manley's murder spree and the Ridge that things would become prosaically normal, that their lives would become quiet, calm. Like most people, not one of them was ever prepared for the changes that lurked around the corners of their lives.

Chapter Nine

As Pea, Trey and Thomas headed to Charlottesville to get a ride on a family friend's private jet, Joseph still sat in the half empty banquet hall, watching the door, still hoping that his wife would walk through it at any moment.

Teri sat next to him and several of his friends from the Bureau were at other tables interviewing the last of the conference attendees and trying to catch the smallest detail that might lead them to what happened. Those attendees not involved directly in law enforcement who had been interviewed had been allowed to leave, but they were afraid as they left. What was happening here, happened to other people, not them, they thought. What Joseph's former co-workers could have told them was that they were "other people", that this could have been one of them just as well.

"Mr. Hallett, do you want someone to drive you home?" Teri asked.

Joseph picked at the table linens and shook his head. He looked around the room at the people still there and tried to recreate in his mind where they had been when Mary had left his side, but all he could see was Mary's receding form, her long hair moving as she walked away. And that made him think of how her hair had swung in they rhythm of their lovemaking that afternoon and he felt a deep pain in his gut. He did not know that tears were threatening to spill over his blonde lashes.

He thought of the hate mail he had kept away from Mary and the rest of the family. The threats contained within them were sick and as demented as the people who wrote them. What was worse were the letters that seemed to relish the gruesome details of his books, asking for more details about the cases.

At first he had read the letters and had stowed them away from everyone. He had thought they had been through enough and didn't need to see some of the filth in those letters. Finally, he took the letters he had received and had sent them to a friend at the Bureau. He stopped opening them and just began to forward what ever came once a month. After the book about the Ridge killers had come out, he had been deluged with the letters and email, but it had slowed down in the last few months.

He watched as his friends from the Bureau continued their work. They might have a step up on this because he had begun sending that correspondence to them. He knew they had a substantial file on him, his family, and even those murderers he had helped to capture before he left to teach at Washington and Lee.

Joseph thought of the first time he had seen Mary sitting in his class in Lexington. She had worn a white and green striped wrap dress and her hair had been pulled back, but even in the midst of all those people, she had been the only one he really saw.

He had spent his first lecture there speaking to her in a sea of listening undergraduates. No one noticed that his focus never left her, but she did and she had smiled at him as if they were the only people there. He was floored by her. He had known so many people in his life, but no one had made him feel the electric shock he felt when she smiled that knowing smile at him.

He didn't know at the time that she wasn't one of his students and so he, following university protocol, did not approach her. But when everyone else was gone, she was still sitting there, waiting for him. She had told him that she wasn't one of his students and that she had slipped into the lecture hall just to hear him speak.

They went to have coffee and spent the rest of the year together. She was graduating from law school that spring and he was completing his guest lectureship as well. Then he had met her sister and Thomas, learned of the murders, the whole bloody mess that resulted in Mary's kidnapping and his heart attack.

He had thought after they had survived that ordeal that they would be okay. And then the Ridge happened. And again, somehow, they had made it through it and he thought they would finally be okay.

Now, it was happening again and Joseph wondered if any of them would ever know a quiet and peaceful life. He sighed and ran his hands through his thinning hair, resting them there and trying to think of everything that had happened this evening once more. No matter how hard he tried, all he could see was Mary.

Jonathan, one of his friends from the Bureau came over to his table and asked him if they could speak to him alone. Joseph waved his hands at the empty seats at the table and nodded.

Teri excused herself and went in search of others working there that she might help.

"Mr. Hallett, I'll be here as long as you need me. Just let me know," she said and walked across the room.

"Joseph," Jonathan said as he sat down, "Are you holding up okay?"

Joseph shrugged his shoulders and continued to sit with his hands clasped across his head.

By that time, three other agents had joined them at the table, each of them holding computer tablets linked to Washington and the files that had been sent from there on Joseph.

Each of them started shooting questions across the table at him and he knew what each question was going to be before they uttered them. He had literally written the book on what they were doing. Except that he hadn't had the little tablets and smart phones when he had been in the field.

He turned to face them at the table and lowered his hands from his head and placed his palms flat on the table. He really needed a drink. Before he began to talk with them, he waved at Teri and held up an empty wine glass. She smiled and nodded, directing one of the remaining wait staff to take a bottle of wine over to the table.

Joseph calmly poured the wine into the empty glass, drained it in one gulp, and then poured more before looking up at the people sitting around him who seemed surprised by his drinking.

"I am not okay. I am fucking five minutes short of either a heart attack or a panic attack," he said and took another drink.

"Joseph, we need you to be clear headed right now, okay," Jonathan said and pointed at the wine.

"My friends, my doctor tells me that red wine is good for my heart and right now it's keeping me calm," he replied.

"My wife appears to have been kidnapped. Again. The last time I let it get to me, I failed her. That – that cannot happen again."

Across the table, one of the female agents he did not know asked him about what they had done the past few days.

He nodded at her and said, "That's a good question. I've been concentrating so hard on this evening and everyone I saw that I hadn't thought about that. You're going to be a good agent."

He raised his glass to her, but did not drink this time. He sat the glass aside.

"Does anyone have a legal pad and pen? I can write out a timeline faster by hand."

Three paper pads instantly appeared in front of him and he smiled wryly.

"Nice to see that some things don't change," he said and began to write an outline of their past few days. When he finished it, he handed it to the female agent who had asked him the question.

"If you don't mind, could you tell me your name again? I know I might have met you earlier, but . . ."

The agent smiled and held her hand out to him. "Tara Spencer. And no, I hadn't had a chance to speak with you before."

He nodded and glanced back to the door. He took a deep breath and looked at the faces around him again.

"Okay, let's start again. Agent Spencer, you're up first."

It was several hours of questions, checking their tablets, calling D.C., and working before they sat back and realized that they still were no farther ahead than they were when they had started. The agents looked at one another furtively, knowing that they were stuck and thinking about Mary's timeline since she disappeared.

"It's okay," Joseph said and this time he picked up the glass and drained it again. "I know how important time is. Hell, I trained two of you."

He looked upward and closed his eyes. Unknown to them, he could hear his Nana Sophia's voice reciting a prayer to St. Jude.

He suddenly stood up and grimly smiled at them.

"It's going to be okay. Pea and Thomas are on their way. And Pea is a force of nature unlike anyone you've ever met. Now, I'm going outside to get a breath of air, if you'll excuse me for a few moments."

As Joseph walked away, he could hear Agent Spencer asking who Pea was. He smiled as he could hear Jonathan say, "Oh, shit."

Oh shit is right, my old friend, Joseph thought. When he thought of Pea, Thomas and Trey coming, he felt hope again.

As he stepped out into the humid Florida air, he could smell the sweetness of Hibiscus blooms on the shrub next to where he stood watching the sky begin to turn a light pink and lavender to the east. He plucked one of the red blooms and held it up, looking a the paper thin petals. He crushed the flower and was in the process of throwing it at the shrubbery when he saw a glint of silver in the mulch at the base of the plant.

He knelt and saw Mary's cell lying there, with Taylor's face dimly glowing on it. He stood and turned to get the agents and thought, Hold on Mary, we're coming. Hold on.

Chapter Ten

Thomas watched the rising sun as the plane landed. He hadn't mentioned it to the others, but for some reason even unknown to him, he had called Diana from his apartment. At first he just pretended to be checking on her, but she had known him too well and he finally told her about Mary. She had been sympathetic and had listened, but she had not offered to be there for him. He could hardly blame her. She was not built for the chaos that always enveloped his life. He asked about her family and then said he had to go. As he hung up the phone, he knew that he had just spoken to Diana for the last time.

Across from him on the plane, Trey was gathering papers together and surreptiously watching Pea sitting opposite him.

Pea's eyes were closed, but both men knew that she was not asleep. They weren't sure what her thoughts were, but they knew where her thoughts were.

Thomas took a deep breath just as the wheels hit the runway and he thought that Pea might be the most dangerous woman he had ever known at that moment. She was so different from the woman he had first known, even the woman who stood next to Mary at the wedding.

But even the first time she had pushed her way into his apartment, he should have known that she was unstoppable, no matter how afraid she seemed. It was as if every challenge made her stronger and braver. If he had known that Joseph had called her a force of nature, he would have laughed and said that she wasn't just a force of nature, she was a fucking hurricane.

"Pea, we're here. There should be a car waiting for us. Jeff said he'd arrange everything for us," Trey said.

Pea opened her eyes and smiled at her husband. They had been so lucky that his friend Jeff Bailey, who owned a horse farm outside of Charlottesville, had been so generous to offer them the use of his private jet, she thought. She looked across the aisle at Thomas and he nodded at her and looked out the window as the plane taxied toward a private hangar.

They stepped out into the heavy humidity of Florida and Pea thought of Ree's pale skin in that horrible heat. How could I have thought that Augusta County was more humid than this, she thought.

"God, I feel like I need a shower just by stepping out into this air," she said as she descended the steps from the plane. "I hope Ree brought sunscreen. Her skin won't take this heat and sun."

Both men stopped behind her in wonderment at her matter of fact tone. Her sister was missing and she was worried about Ree's skin. It's as if she knows Mary's still alive, Trey thought. He looked at Thomas and just shrugged his shoulders. Thomas was mute. He was always surprised by Pea and her statement gave him reason to hope.

They arrived at the university thirty minutes later and Pea was out of the car heading into the building before the car had completely stopped. Inside, Joseph was still sitting where he had been most of the night. There were still agents and officers there and one of the campus security guards tried to stop Pea as she rushed into the room. She pushed past his six foot four heavy build as if she could walk through brick walls. Everyone in the room stopped what they were doing to watch the thin blonde storm into the room and cross the room toward Joseph.

Joseph stood and ran to her, embracing her and burying his head in her blonde hair. His body shook as he finally released the grief and fear that he had been holding back through the long night.

Trey and Thomas entered and watched as Pea comforted Joseph while everyone stood around looking at her in amazement. Trey heard one of the men derisively tell a woman that "the fucking force of nature had arrive." Trey ignored the man and walked to his wife and Joseph.

Thomas had heard the comment as well, but he paused and softly said to the man, "Yes, you're fucking right, but if I hear you talk about her like that again, you'll be swallowing your teeth."

Just as one of the younger agents was about to say something Jonathan knew would be stupid, Thomas walked away. Jonathan silenced the agent and looked at the group across from them.

Suddenly, he actually believed that things might be okay. The four of them together looked unbreakable, and he had to admit, Joseph's sister-in-law was fucking magnificent. She appeared formidable. Then he thought of her past – her facing down her ex-husband with the barrel of a shotgun she had pulled to her chest and her taking down the Redemption Ridge killers. He wondered where that ability to face death came from. Had he known her full history, he would never have thought twice about it.

Jonathan gave them a few minutes before nodding for his team to follow him and walk to where the four stood.

Joseph had calmed and turned to introduce his family to the agents and officers.

They all quickly shook hands and began to take seats around the large banquet table.

"Pea, she was so afraid last night. It's my fault. I'm sorry. I should have listened to her. You both have always known when things were wrong. I should have listened. I was such an idiot," Joseph said.

"Joseph, we all know you had to get her away. You couldn't know this would happen. Don't blame yourself. Blame the bastard who took her. We'll find her and god help him when we do," Pea said tersely.

Trey took Pea's hand in his to make her aware of the people surrounding them. She suddenly acknowledged them and closed her mouth, meeting her husband's eyes and silently understanding his touch.

"Joseph, did anything happen yesterday that might have made you think twice?" Thomas asked.

Some of the agents looked at Thomas in surprise, but Jonathan did not. He knew Thomas's history as well. Joseph had confided in him about all of them, including Thomas. Jonathan knew that Thomas was not to be underestimated, either. Besides, he looked like a Navy Seal. Strong and intelligent and unstoppable.

Joseph appeared so tired that Pea looked to Jonathan as if she knew he was in charge.

"When did he eat last? Has he rested at all?" she asked.

Trey squeezed her hand again.

"I'm sorry," she said to Jonathan and then turned to Joseph.

"Joseph, you're not going to do Ree any good if you get sick. I'm sorry. I'm worried about you, too."

Joseph leaned back in the chair.

"You're right. I just couldn't eat. I don't think I could rest as long as she's missing."

The young male agent asked one of the others, "Who's Ree? I thought his wife's name was Mary."

Jonathan glared at him and he was chastened enough to step away from the table. Jonathan was starting to think that keeping him here was a mistake.

"Thomas," Joseph said. "To answer your question, let me think. We arrived here early yesterday afternoon. Talked to some people. Uh, at one point we got separated, but I could see her nearby."

Thomas leaned forward and looked down at the table linens.

"Who else was here beside the conference people?" he asked.

Joseph thought for a minute, trying to remember anyone he might have missed.

"Well, there was Teri, who's in charge of everything. She would know everyone's name who was working . . . wait, there was one man. Really tall. He stared at Mary for a long time. Enough that I noticed it."

"I think he works here. He was pushing a cleaning cart around."

Joseph closed his eyes and tried to remember the man.

He kept his eyes closed as he began to speak again.

"I think he was wearing sort of grayish green work clothes. Had the university logo on his shirt on one side and his name on . . ."

"Shit, I can't remember what name was on the shirt," he said and opened his eyes. "But I do remember he was very tall, about 6'6" tall and extremely thin, sort of gaunt, about 45, maybe."

He stopped and took a second and looked around the room.

"Is Teri still here? I think she was talking to him as we were leaving. He had . . . damn, Thomas! He had tablecloths in his arms. How could I forget that? He looked like a fucking undertaker. He was working here. And he couldn't take his eyes off of Mary."

Joseph turned to Jonathan. "Can you get someone to see if Teri is still here? She would know his name. Can someone get Teri?" Joseph said and stood, looking frantically around the room.

Pea placed her hand on Joseph's arm and gently led him to sit again. His hands were visibly shaking. He looked up at Pea and Trey.

"The whole time I thought this had something to do with those whackos. My damn ego. I never thought that it might have just been about Mary. Shit. I've wasted hours," he said.

Thomas stood and placed his hand on Joseph's shoulder.

"You're not superman, Joseph. Remember what you told me about Shawnette? Remember? Look, I'm going to go get food from somewhere for you. You have to eat. Okay?"

Joseph looked up at Thomas and smiled his thanks.

Thomas headed toward the door and Jonathan called out to him to stop. Thomas waited and Jonathan approached him, waving the young male agent over and one of the campus cops.

Pea couldn't hear what was being said, but she could see Jonathan talking quickly and the three men nodding as he spoke. The young agent quickly went out the door and the campus cop followed him as Jonathan and Thomas came back to the table.

"I've delegated some things. We need Thomas here. He's made more progress than we have by asking the right questions. A fact I have to sadly admit that we failed to do. Questions we should have thought of if we hadn't been so busy checking everyone attending the conference."

"Joseph, if I can get a sketch artist here, do you feel up to working with him? It would go a long way, especially if he's working under an alias. Someone in Orlando has to have seen this guy outside the campus if he's as distinctive as you say."

Joseph nodded and lay his head down on his arms on the table.

Without raising his head he said, "Was Taylor okay? Mary was so worried." His voice broke slightly when he said Mary's name.

Pea placed her hand on Joseph's back and began to rub it.

"Taylor's fine, Joseph. She and the boys are home. The Franklins are there and Dan sent over a deputy to stay until Mary's home," she said.

Trey grimaced. Dan had lost a good deputy the last time. The best they could hope for this time was that whoever had taken Mary was working alone and still here. He hated to think that the death that seemed to follow them would find their children.

But Dan had made the offer the minute Trey had called him and told him that Mary was missing in Florida. Trey thought that Dan was a good man and a good policeman. And the good ones were always the ones who were ignored by the media. His train of thought returned to Florida and Mary.

"It's all going to be okay, Joseph. Rest for a few. We'll find her," Pea continued.

She looked to Trey and Thomas and smiled.

"She's alive. I know. She's okay."

Trey and Thomas returned her smile. If she said so, if she said so.

Chapter Eleven

Mary was alive, but she woke to darkness and the stench of rot. She started to sit up and found that she could not raise her head. She tried to open her mouth to speak, but something bit into her jaw and dug into her neck when she tried to move her jaw.

Her arms were free and she raised them to find some kind of iron pipe with jagged edges around her throat. She touched her side and realized she was nude. She began to panic and tried to lift the pipe with her hands so she could at least sit up, but the pipe was too heavy and every attempt she made to lift it was agony.

She was on the verge of screaming even if the thing cut her throat when she heard a soft whisper nearby.

"Don't move too . . . much. It might slice your jug . . . jugular. Try to breathe slowly."

It was a woman's voice coming from the left of her body.

"Where . . am I? What's . . ?" Mary managed to whisper without moving her jaw. Part of what she said sounded like gibberish to her ears.

There are no sound for a few seconds and then the woman whispered again, her words measured and slow.

"I don't know. I was running in Cady Way Park when I tripped. I woke up here. He's not here now. We can whisper. But . . . when he's, don't talk. Don't move and," the voice paused as if the woman was in great pain. "Try not to open your eyes, no matter what you hear."

Mary tried to take in what the woman's voice was telling her. She tried to remember how she got here. She remembered her nakedness and panicked again. Oh, god, have I been . . . She could not finish the thought.

The heat and smell of this place was unbearable, but her eyes were beginning to adjust to the small amount of light coming through the walls and ceiling. She couldn't turn her head, but she could see up and some things in front of her and from the corners of her eyes.

She could feel that she was on some kind of cloth camping cot and she could hear breathing other than her own and that of the woman next to her.

"Who are you? Is there anyone else here?" Mary asked. It was difficult to talk without moving her mouth, but she was slowly learning to do it.

Again, the woman was slow in answering and her voice was more garbled than Mary and sounded weaker.

"Naomi. Yes, two others. One Ruth. One." She paused and struggled to continue. "One Eve."

Mary could hear a soft moan across the room.

"Who's that?" Mary asked.

"Eve," the woman said. Again a long pause. "He hurt her . . . bad last night. Night. Lantern. Could see. Prays."

Mary listened closely. The moans sounded as if the woman were dying. What did Naomi mean "prays"?

"Prays? Who?"

"He. Angels. Calls us. Angels." Naomi managed to get out.

Mary could feel sweat on her skin. She knew she would not last long in this heat. She would lose her strength quickly. She had to figure a way out of here before "he" came back. She slowly ran her hand across the face of the pipe and found a lock on the right side in the center. It was a keyed lock. If she could somehow pick the lock, she could get the pipe off, but there was nothing near her nude body.

She suddenly thought of the single diamond stud and hoop earrings Joseph had given her after Taylor's birth. They had long posts and were platinum. She reached up to her ear and found them still in her ears. She wondered if the posts would be long enough to use on the lock or if she could bend the hoops to lengthen them.

It seemed to take hours to work the screw backs from the earrings with one hand before she finally got one loose enough to pull the hoop from her ear. She could touch most of her body with both hands, but the iron teeth bit into her shoulder blades when she did. She could feel liquid trickling down her chest and wondered if it was blood or sweat or both.

As she worked on the hoop, she could hear the woman called Eve gasping for breath.

She stopped for a moment and listened as Eve's moans were louder. It also sounded as if there was some sort of rattling sound coming from her with each breath.

"Naomi, is she okay?"

Naomi sighed and murmured "No."

"What happened?"

Naomi was silent.

Mary began to fear that Naomi might be in bad shape as well.

Finally Naomi got the words "Don't ask" out. Then she surprised Mary by continuing to speak.

"He tortures us. Slowly. Seven days with each, with each thing. But . . . until last, last night . . . never rape. Raped Eve. Hurt her."

Mary began to become deathly afraid of her situation and started to work on the hoop as Naomi started whispering again.

"I've been . . . four days. Collar. Then the leather. Hanging. Next. Then something with water outside. One woman, didn't know her name . . . never came back. Each one seven days. Final . . . " her voice faltered.

"Three days before . . ."

Mary could hear Naomi crying. She realized that whatever had been done to Eve would be done to Naomi in three days. Then she was hit with the fact that she would follow Naomi.

She looked up at the sunlight coming through the cracks in the roof and thought of Joseph and Taylor.

Hell, no, she would not be lost to them. She would either be found or she would escape. If she could live through Manley's rape, she could get through this. For the first time since that night, she was angry and defiant as she had not been since she had discovered Manley sitting in his car in front of her apartment.

What Pea and the others never knew was that Manley had repeatedly raped her on the kitchen floor before they found the farmhouse in Goshen. He had sneered at her and beat her with his fists. When he had chained her to the sink, he pushed her face into the old linoleum and had spread her legs so far that she thought they would break.

Manley raped her twice, telling her what he was going to do to her later in detail, including removing a different body part every time he fucked her. He then inexplicably had stopped. He had dressed, kicked her hard in the stomach and smiled as if he had a new toy.

He left her there and made a sandwich while she curled up on the floor, her body so weak she could not move. He had talked as he ate and told her of the women he had brought here and what he had done to them. What he described terrified her, drained her of the will to live, and made her contemplate suicide. He had told her that he had given them a nerve block, but he wasn't going to do that to her.

He had said, "I want you to feel everything, every second, bitch. I can't wait," and had continued to chew his food, crunching potato chips with the sandwich.

After finishing eating, he had gotten the tool kit out and was about to use a hammer handle with which to rape her when he had heard the car outside.

"Ah, as I had hoped. The "cavalry" has arrived. Your cunt of a sister knows what I'll do to her after I kill your other friends. I cannot wait. Having both of you in my basement, oh, what fun we'll have."

He tossed the hammer back into the tool kit.

"Guess that will have to wait. Probably should get the shotgun. That's a thought. I could use it, too. Bet you've never had a shotgun inside you. Lots of things around here you've probably never had," he had said and had gone in search of his shotgun.

Mary had just crawled into a ball next to the sink when Pea had entered.

The rest, of course, resulted in Manley's death and Thomas being shot, but when she had learned that Joseph had had a heart attack, she had never mentioned the rape. She had decided she would tell him later, but the more time passed, the less she was able to talk about Goshen and she had found herself withdrawing into her fear until she felt nothing but shame.

She still made love to Joseph after that, but every time, she found that smile was getting harder to produce. When she had become pregnant, she felt she might be delivered from the nightmare, but that, of course, did not happen and she became a shell of the woman who had stared across that auditorium at Joseph, daring him to match her gaze.

Now, she was kidnapped again, possibly again in preparation for torture and death. But, this time she would not give up. She could not stop seeing Joseph and Taylor. She had to live for them, she thought. She could not give up. It was then that she heard Eve's breathing stop and she clinched her fists.

No, she screamed inwardly. No! No! No! I will not die this way! I will see my husband and my baby again.

"I think . . . Eve," Naomi struggled to speak.

"I know," Mary said. She could see quite a lot of the cabin now and realized that it must be nearing noon by the amount of sunlight in the room.

For the first time she could see the poster boards papering the cabin walls. They were filled with scrawled prayers, rules, drawings of what looked like torture devices, and lists of procedures to be followed. The ones she could see all ended with the phrase, "So saith the Lord."

Naomi had said he called them angels. Did he believe they were angels? She thought about Joseph's lectures she had attended, about how serial rapists and killers followed certain routines obsessively. This guy seemed to be beyond that.

Oh great, I've been kidnapped by a religious nut who has OCD, she thought and giggled crazily. She realized she was in shock. The situation was more than she could comprehend and she began trying to work the platinum hoop into something she could use to remove the lock from the pipe.

Teri had stayed at the banquet hall as long as she physically could. When she saw that she was no longer functioning on no food and no sleep and that Joseph's family had arrived, she slipped out the door and headed to her car to try to get a few hours sleep and a hot shower.

She was so exhausted that she failed to see Raymond Templeton in the car window as he approached from behind her with a chloroformed pad that he stuffed in her mouth and nose. Her last thought as she slipped to the ground was that she should have told Joseph about Templeton and how he frightened her.

Raymond dragged her into the brush around the parking lot and shoved her into his white maintenance van. As he drove his Mary back to his cabin earlier, he had seen that Teri would eventually tell the police about him. She would lead them straight to him.

But after getting Mary settled in and placing her collar on her sleeping body, he drove back to the campus to get Teri and his personnel records from the HR office. His only advantage of being in maintenance – keys to their kingdom. He knew that the police might figure out he was an employee, but without Teri or his file, they might not, either.

The only thing that worried him was that he had to leave his car near the campus and use the maintenance van to move Teri. He would make quick work of her and then drive back to where his car was parked and switch vehicles. He thought that he would have to wipe the van down before returning it. He didn't want to risk leaving any evidence.

As he drove to his house, he could hear Teri waking in the back of the van. She was just about to start to scream when he took a pipe wrench from the passenger seat and swung it back against the top of her head. After that, the ride was peacefully quiet. He saw that the day was going to be a beautiful Florida day filled with sunshine.

Thank you, Lord, for this is the day you have made for me, he thought and began whistling as he drove home.

Mary heard the van outside and Naomi's breathing began to quicken. Mary could tell that she was terrified. Maybe she thought that Eve's death would move her own torture faster along.

"Naomi, calm down. Men like him stick to routines. Look at the walls. He won't break his idea of god's rules," Mary whispered, pausing to try to moisten her mouth but was having difficulty producing saliva.

She began to understand that she was becoming dehydrated and tried to think of what she could use to suck on to moisten her mouth. She remembered the diamond hoop in her hand and popped it into her mouth, moving it around the inside of her mouth with her tongue. It helped a bit, but not much.

She was about to remove it from her mouth when Raymond opened the door and blinding light flooded the cabin. He left the door open and walked back outside and for the first time she could see most of the cabin, including the leather harness and pulley system on the overhead beam in the center of the room. She shivered as she could only imagine what he might use it for.

She slipped the earring out of her mouth and placed it back in her ear, praying that it would not fall out and give her away when he returned from outside the cabin. As she finished with the earring she saw the other three cots.

Naomi, who was next to her, had bright copper red hair. Her body looked like it was once strong, but now appeared thin. If he starved them, he would use that to further weaken them, she thought. She believed that Naomi's body was beginning to turn on itself in order to keep her heart going. If he began her torture with the harness in three days, he might kill her.

Mary then could barely make out the shapes of Ruth and Eve on cots across from her. Mary was surprised to see that the other women were redheads as well. She thought that would make sense to his pathology, as Joseph would have said. Ruth was much worse than Naomi, but she was still breathing. Eve no longer breathed. Her pain had ended abruptly this morning.

"God, help Joseph find me," she prayed. She could see Joseph's face in her mind and momentarily despaired of ever seeing it again. Then she thought of Taylor and her resolve to escape strengthened again.

Mary noticed that Naomi and Ruth both closed their eyes and were motionless after the door had opened. She tried to mimic their postures, but she did try to keep her eyelids slightly open so she could see the man who had brought them there.

The man suddenly came through the door dragging a woman by her hair that was matted with what Mary thought was oil and then saw was dark blood in the sunlight.

He was quoting scripture about Sodom and Gomorrah and the great whore of Babylon as he began stripping the woman's clothes off.

He stopped for a moment and looked at the women on the cots.

"My angels, please do not watch the punishment I must mete out upon this mortal whore. She would have prevented our ascension and she is a tool of the devil."

Our ascension? Mary involuntarily shivered. She had attended church until her confirmation at 12 and then had slowly drifted toward other pursuits. She had continued to attend occasionally with her parents until their deaths and then had left the church and religion behind her.

But she remembered enough from her confirmation classes to know what he was referring to when he said the word ascension. What terrified her was his use of the pronoun "our",

The man continued with his tasks without looking at her or the other cots. He lowered the harness and placed the dark haired girl into it. The girl was waking up just as her arms were jerked upward behind her back hard and quickly.

She was about to scream when the man began to stuff dirty rags in her mouth. Her eyes were wide with fear and pain as she barely managed to stay on her tiptoes to keep the straps from dislocating her shoulders.

Mary watched in horror as she recognized Teri, the conference organizer from yesterday. Mary bit her lip as she also recognized the man as the janitor she had smiled at yesterday.

She watched the janitor begin to turn the lever that was raising Teri upward. Even with the gag, Mary could hear her muffled screams.

Oh, my god, my god, help her, Mary prayed.

But no one appeared to stop the man and Mary watched his back as he raped Teri's limp body, first with his penis and then with some sort of metal thing that looked like a pear. As he pushed it into Teri, he masturbated while he continued to pray loudly. By the time he squirted semen on her feet, blood was pouring from her body. He raised her a little higher removed the pear thing which looked like an open metal flower now and began to lick the blood on her thighs, sucking at her as he were drinking Teri's blood.

It was when he began chewing at Teri's legs that Mary fully opened her eyes and saw that Teri was still alive and feeling the man literally tearing her flesh away. Mary began to feel vomit rise in her throat and knew she would choke on it. She took one last look at Teri's face, and then closed her eyes and mercifully passed out from the shock of what she had just witnessed

Chapter Twelve

The young male agent found Teri's car and purse with her cell phone in the parking lot behind the auditorium. He felt a cold sweat break across his forehead and began to run back to the banquet hall. Now there were two women missing. It was only a matter of time before the media arrived and he thought that they were screwed for sure.

As he ran into the hall, he was so out of breath that he had to stop at the door for a second. Jonathan and the other agents hurried over to him and listened as he sputtered out the details of what he had found.

Jonathan looked over at the table where Joseph and his family sat and shook his head. Joseph knew that somehow things had just gotten worse and he closed his eyes and silently began to recite the prayer to St. Jude.

"Something bad has happened," Thomas said and walked over to where the agents were gathered. He listened to them in shock and returned to the table.

"Tell me it's not Mary," Joseph whispered.

Thomas sat down and placed a hand on his friend's shoulder.

"No, not Mary, but they think the woman, Teri, has been taken, too. They found her purse and car out in the lot. There was a small amount of blood on the ground and the car. They think it may be from where she hit her legs on the car trying to kick at whoever took her."

Trey looked at Pea and began to be afraid for her now. This man was crazier than anyone they had faced before. Two women in one night? There was no way he was going to allow Pea out of his sight, he thought.

Pea could see the determination set in on Trey's face and she knew what that meant. He wanted to be the strong one for her, but he was the gentlest among them, she thought. His childhood haunted him and although he had helped her to escape her own self-imposed prison, he did not see his own fears as an impediment.

She then looked at Thomas who did not turn from her gaze. He knew what she knew – that the world they lived in most days was an illusion of safety, that the real world, without the smoke and mirrors of self-deception, was treacherous, dangerous, and deadly.

She leaned her head against Trey's shoulder, but continued to stare at Thomas. She had known from the moment that she had walked into his apartment that they both had seen what no one should ever see. They had seen the world stripped, bare, and cold.

It had been enough for Thomas to unwittingly drive Diana from his side, she thought. She nestled against Trey and sighed. Trey refused to see anything beyond his love for her and his sons and their quiet existence in Augusta County. The rest of the world existed only in the illusion of what he thought of as a good place with good people.

She turned to look at Joseph who continued to stare at the door. She thought that they needed to get him out of here. He was key to helping find Mary and he was useless to anyone right now.

"Joseph," she said, "Perhaps we could go back to where you and Ree were staying and you could sleep for a little bit."

Joseph turned to her and shook his head. He could not get back in that bed where he and Mary had spent their last few hours together making love. The thought of doing so made him a little crazy.

"No, no, I need to work."

He looked around the room and called out to Jonathan.

"Can we get some kind of erasable board in here or something like it.?"

He looked to Pea, Thomas, and Trey.

"We need to look at this as a whole picture, the way we did . . ." he broke off thinking of Mary's picture on a board instead of Shawnette's and understood for the first time in his career the unbearable anguish the families and lovers of victims endured when he had investigated them.

"As we did with Shawnette," Thomas finished for him. His deep voice was powerful even when he spoke quietly.

"I'm sorry, Thomas. I never knew how, how this felt for you."

He began to pace near them a little manically.

"I have to do something. I cannot sit here. I can't sleep."

He stopped and looked to Pea.

"You know. You know why and how. We've done this before. We can do it again," he said resting his hands on the back of his empty chair.

"Yes, Joseph, but we had time. We rested. We ate," she said. "Our fears for Ree change everything. We need to be more, more proactive, I suppose."

Trey disengaged his arm from Pea and stared in horror at Joseph. He shook his head, looked to Pea and saw that she was in agreement with Joseph.

He stood and pointed his finger at Joseph.

"You are too close to this. And you two," he said to Pea and Thomas, "you two have almost died twice from this kind of shit. I know it's Mary and you think that makes it different, but it really makes it worse."

Now he spoke to Pea.

"How can you think of putting your sister's picture on a board and treating this as some puzzle you have to solve. For fuck's sake, Pea, you do not have to repent for Alicia's death over and over again!"

Pea was taken aback by Trey's vehemence. Could he not see that she was lost without Ree? How could he act this way in front of Joseph?

Pea stood and faced him. She spoke in a whisper as she placed her hand upon his cheek. She could see wisps of grey in his black curls. She wished she could made him understand how deep her love was for him and how it made her even more determined to find her sister.

"Ree is our family. Your family, now, too. I am not repenting anything. I am doing this because this is our family, because of Joseph and Taylor and our boys and Thomas. I do it because I cannot not do it."

Trey leaned his face against Pea's hand and kissed her palm. He nodded and pulled her close to him and whispered into her ear.

"I just can't lose you. Please. Be careful. Please," he said and then kissed her forehead and stepped away from the table to leave the three of them.

Thomas watched his retreating form. He knew Trey's fears, but he understood Pea and Joseph's needs.

"He'll be back, Pea," he said.

"I know. He just needs some room right now," she replied as she sat while watching Trey leave the hall. "But we need the stuff Joseph asked for and I'm going to find that Jonathan man and get it."

Before she could rise from her seat, she saw the agents wheeling in two large boards that were already covered with photos and writing. They had kept the boards away from the family because it was policy that the victim's families never see them. But Jonathan has reasoned that this time, this abduction was outside policy and he did something that he, that most agents, never did – he threw out the rules and put the family right in the middle of everything.

Joseph, Pea and Thomas stood together and began to walk the lengths of the boards, studying everything there, every comment, every lead.

"Where's the map?" Thomas asked.

Jonathan was surprised by his astuteness.

"We use the tablets now," he said and handed Thomas his tablet with a map of the Orlando area on it.

Thomas studied it as Pea and Joseph continued reading the boards. They stopped suddenly at Thomas's next words.

"What are these other red dots? Especially the ones in this area? Is this a park?"

Both Pea and Joseph looked at the tablet and Pea gasped at what she saw. Over 20 red dots were on the screen.

"Oh, you bastards," Joseph said and rushed at Jonathan. He managed to get a solid connection with Jonathan's jaw before Thomas pulled him back.

"How long have you known this?" he spit at him. "You invited me and my wife and knew that there was a serial killer here. How could you do that? I thought you were my friend."

Jonathan sat down in a nearby chair and rubbed his face where Joseph's fist had landed. The other agents stood to the side, rooted in place, not knowing how to act or what to say.

"I should have told you. I was going to bring it up during the conference, pick your brain about it. I didn't think you'd come if I told you the real reason," he said.

He lowered his head and looked at the high polish on his shoes.

"I'm really sorry. I had no idea your wife had red hair. I never thought for an instant that she might be in danger. It's my fault and I am so very sorry."

Joseph put his hands on his hips and paced back and forth in front of the boards.

"You're damn right it's your fault. If you . . . Wait, the other victims are red heads? What the fuck is the matter with you, Jon?" Joseph said and rushed at the agent again and again was restrained by Thomas, who held his arms as Joseph struggled to get to the man.

Joseph suddenly collapsed into a chair and buried his face in his hands. Thomas looked at Jonathan with disgust and hatred. He was astounded that the man had used Joseph the way he had.

Pea had observed the entire exchange and had waited patiently for them to calm down. She took a deep breath, exhaled slowly and looked venomously at Jonathan.

"We need all the information on all the victims. Everything. Photos. Connections. Anything. Now."

Trey had come back into the hall just in time to witness everything. He watched as his wife took over and he leaned against the door frame. He thought of their twins and then of Taylor. Taylor. What if they didn't find Mary in time? Taylor would grow up motherless and alone as he had and for the first time he felt the urgency to fix this, too.

He briskly joined his wife and stared at the agents.

"She's right. We need everything now. Somebody needs to get it or the media will know everything faster than you can think," he said,

Thomas joined them as they stood behind Joseph and formed a wall in front of the agents.

Jonathan sighed. They were not going to give up and he knew his failure to tell Joseph everything made him complicit in Mary's abduction.

"Get them everything, including a paper map of the area," he said and leaned back into the chair.

In for a penny, in for a pound, he thought and laid his hand upon the table

.

Chapter Thirteen

It took the agents and Joseph's group over two hours to put everything together in the order that Joseph wanted. The other agents, unfamiliar with Joseph's methodology as it did not use the technology they had come to depend on, were slower in seeing connections that even Trey saw and he had never really done this sort of thing. He had been absent from the time Joseph, Pea, and Thomas had searched for Shawnette's killer.

Looking back, he felt as if he had been blind to everything but his love for Pea during that time. He realized now how seriously close he had come to losing her then and he now felt the fear that Thomas had lived through and that Joseph was trying to endure.

He wondered if he could be as strong for Pea as they were and had been for the women they had lost. He heard the past tense in his head and tried to shake it off. Not yet. Mary was still alive. Pea was so sure of it that he had to trust her instincts. With the exception of her blind belief in Manley, her instincts had been right in the past.

Joseph tried to talk to Pea and Thomas about patterns and connections he saw, but the newer agents kept interrupting him with questions.

Suddenly he threw the marker in his hand across the room and shouted at them.

"Will you shut the fuck up? This is not a master class in profiling. This is my wife. Let me work. Stay out of our way and just shut up."

He turned to the board and his shoulders sagged. His outburst embarrassed him and he faced them again.

"Listen, I'm sorry. It's just there's only so much time. Please. Understand. I'm not trying to be rude. I just need you to let me think. Don't speak unless you see something that I'm missing. Okay?"

They all sat and nodded. They had separated themselves from Jonathan, who sat at another table, alone and musing on his stupidity that had resulted not only in his friend losing his wife, but the kidnapping of another woman the same night. And that was when he made the connection of Teri with Mary.

"Joseph," he called out. "Why would he take Teri? She's not his type. She's dark haired. There's no real reason for it unless . . ."

Joseph's face lit up.

"Unless she knew something she didn't realize she knew. And the man knew that."

He looked to the agents.

"Can you get all the HR files? Including the paper files?"

They all scrambled out of the room to get to the personnel records and bring what they could back to the hall. One agent stayed behind and tried to connect with the HR computer through a laptop and not a tablet.

"I might be able to access their database if I can get through. There might be information there, that is if you want me to try," he said to Joseph.

Joseph nodded and said, "Yes, of course, anything that might help."

He turned to his friends.

"If only I could figure out what Teri knew that she didn't know she knew. I keep staring at these women, but all I can see is Mary."

As he spoke, he began to lose his balance and Trey was quick to grab his arm as Thomas moved to help him. He was fading fast, Thomas thought. He remembered the sofa in the lobby and thought that if they could get Joseph to rest for just a few minutes.

"Trey, he's got to rest. His heart might not be able to take this. Can you help me move the sofa in the lobby into one of the side rooms?"

"Yeah," Trey said. "There's a classroom across from this hall. That would be good. Pea, can you stay with him until we get things done?"

Joseph was eerily silent throughout their conversation. As they left, he took from his belt loop a small white cylinder and removed a brown glass bottle from it. Pea knew he was getting a nitro tablet. His hands were shaking and she placed hers over his and took the bottle from him and unscrewed the lid.

"Ree told me what the white cylinder was. She wanted to make sure I knew in case she wasn't home and you needed it."

Joseph gave her a weak smile and took a tablet from the glass bottle. Here comes the headache, he thought, but my chest won't feel like someone's pounding on it.

By the time Pea had replaced the bottle back into the cylinder and had put it back on his side belt loop, she could see the color returning to his face. She had no idea it worked that quickly, but she was relieved that it did. They needed Joseph to save Ree and they could not have him in the hospital again.

"Joseph, I'm not going to argue with you about this. You have to do it for Ree. You have to go with Trey and Thomas and try to rest for at least an hour or two. You're no good to her or us otherwise."

He nodded and took her arm as she led him to Trey and Thomas who were returning.

Before she handed him over to them, she took his hand in hers again.

"I promise to wake you up in a few hours. Then you'll eat and we look at everything together again. I promise."

As her husband and Thomas walked with Joseph to the room across from the hall where he had spent the last 20 hours, she sat in front of the boards and began to study them again. The answer was there, just as it had been in the past. Unlike the ridge, there would be no blind serendipity to finding Ree, of stumbling upon one of the killers by accident, it would have to be a matter of looking at each case and somehow finding the commonalities between them all.

Except for the woman named Teri, she thought. And Teri, she thought, was probably already dead or would be very soon. The person doing this had no use for her. She was an inconvenience for him, for his purposes, whatever they might be.

God help her, Pea thought. I hope her passing is not too painful.

Chapter Fourteen

Teri's passing was horrible beyond anything that Manley had ever done to his victims. The pain of the backward suspension of hanging her by her arms behind her body, the rape first by the man who haunted her nightmares, and then the pear that cut her insides apart, they were all mere preludes to feeling the monster below her as he tore at the flesh of her thighs with his teeth, sometimes pulling long strips of skin and muscle away and spitting them onto the floor, and sometimes sucking the blood from the wounds and taking small, but deeper bites from her that he chewed and swallowed.

As he did this to her, he recited the liturgy of communion between bites and suckling where her genitalia had once been. He did it slowly and purposefully. Once he stopped and looked up into her eyes and spoke.

"This is the only way your sins can be redeemed and your whoring ways be forgiven. Only by this can you be welcomed into heaven."

Teri tried to kick at him to keep him from completing his idea of communion but she was unaware that her legs no longer would move. Her brain sent commands that went unresponsive except for the return message of pain. She knew she was dying and she prayed that death come quickly. But he stopped her futile struggles by merely taking each foot and tying it the post. She was left hanging forward as if she were the masthead of a sailing ship, except that he had separated her legs by tying each foot to a different side of the post and giving him just enough room to continue his work.

Before recommencing his task, he looked to his four angels who seemed to be sleeping, as silent as stone statues. It was then that he realized that Eve was not just immobile, but was no longer breathing. He rushed to her and felt her cold body that was already beginning to stiffen in death.

Her body, which had slowly bled out from the injuries she received during the assault of the previous night, was white like that of a statue. Raymond could now see only the silvery gleam of her wings and the fire of her halo of red hair. The rest if her body was void of any color. Even her eyes were clouded.

He howled in anguish.

If he had not been so involved in saving the whore, he might have saved his angel, he thought. He looked to Teri with hatred and then lay his angel Eve back upon the cot, but not before taking a key from the key ring on his belt and unlocking the collar, removing it, and spreading her hair to complete a perfect halo around her face.

Although she had died before the pressing and the pear and the water tests, she was still his angel as he reasoned that God had revealed his plan for his Mary through the angel Eve.

After he finished with the whore, he would take his Eve to join her fellow angels and the whore to the swamp. Although he was not nor had ever been Catholic, he had adopted their sign of the cross and the words of their last rites. This he did for his angel Eve and he kissed her white lips.

He then rose and returned to Teri, who had watched him. She began to scream through the gag even before he reached her. She knew his communion was about to begin again and she knew that she had no escape from him. Her body convulsed as she continued screaming, finally seizing from the fear and pain. The last thing she was aware of was his biting deep into her femoral artery and watching as her life blood covered his naked, thin body in a film of bright red.

Mary had awoken when the man had discovered Eve's dead body and had howled like a wounded animal as he held her in his arms.

She watched as he took the key ring on his belt and tried to see which key he used to remove the collar from Eve. If she could get her hands on that key ring, she might have another chance at surviving if she couldn't pick the lock.

Looking a Teri's hanging body and seeing that she was still awake and aware of the shredded lower half of her body made her even more determined to escape. She closed her eyes as he completed his work with Teri and lay as still as Naomi and Ruth did. Better to be a stone angel than a dead one.

She tried not to think about how Eve had died or how Teri was dying in the room next to her cot. She instead thought of her home in Greenbrier County, her wedding to Joseph, the birth of Taylor, Taylor's first words and first steps. Taylor. Joseph.

Mary suddenly thought of the lists of rules that papered the walls of the cabin. There was something there that was nagging at her mind. She opened her eyes and tried to focus on the walls rather than the horror show going on before her eyes.

She found the list that had "Angel Prerequisites" written in large letters next to the door. She shivered as she read them and realized that they could describe her. Red hair. Blonde sometimes allowed. Healthy. Young. Intelligent. Pure. Winged. Winged? She asked herself. Did this nut job think they had wings? Childless. Married females were allowed. Biblical names.

She stopped and went back up the list: childless. She had a child. If he hurt her, he would be breaking his own weird covenant with his idea of whom God was. Somehow she had to get him to understand that she had given birth to a living child, who, thank God, she thought, was over a thousand miles away. Could the existence of Taylor save her or at least change what he had planned for what he had termed "their ascension"? It was almost too much to hope for, but she had come to the point that she would grab onto anything that would keep her alive.

She closed her eyes again, but she could tell that Teri's torture was over. No more sounds came from her and the noises the man was making sounded as if he were lowering the woman's body and removing the leather device from her.

Mary kept quiet and dared not look at him. Right now she wanted to do nothing to attract his attentions toward her. If, as Naomi had told her, he did follow a regimen of seven days for each part of their torture, then she was on day one of what appeared to be the less painful part of the ordeal, she thought,

Taylor, Joseph, I love you. I'll love you forever. Find me, Joseph. Find me, she prayed, hoping that somewhere in Orlando he might be one step closer to her, one step closer for her to see him, to see Taylor again.

Chapter Fifteen

Pea had lain her head down on her arm and dozed off as she stared at the women and the information on the boards. It had all started to blur and she finally stopped trying to snap back awake and gave in to sleep.

She dreamed of Ree as a child and saw Ree playing in the backyard of the Greenbrier farm with Alicia. They giggled together and Alicia looked up and spoke to her.

"Mommy, don't we look alike? We can grow wings and run. Watch us run, Mommy!"

Little Ree followed her niece in a circle around the yard.

"Come and find me, Pea," she said. "Tell Joseph to come, too. Angels can fly. We can fly."

Pea jerked awake and stood so quickly that her chair flew backwards from where she now stood.

Trey and Thomas were sitting at the table across from her, each of them eating food the campus officer had returned with. They looked up in shock at her sudden wakefulness.

"Pea, hon, are you okay?" Trey asked.

She ignored him and went to the boards. Running. Wings. She went from face to face, reading the descriptions again, this time with an idea of something to look for.

"I found it! I found it!" she yelled.

Both men dropped their sandwiches and ran to flank her before the boards.

"The women had a few things in common – red heads, below 30 years in age, and they were all runners! They all ran, probably in that park you mentioned with the red dots, Thomas."

"Can we replicate those dots of this map and connect them to where the women lived and worked the way Joseph did with Manley's victims?" she asked.

Trey grabbed one of the tablets from the agents without asking and opened it to the map. Meanwhile, Thomas had grabbed a box of push pins and was ready to place one with each location Trey gave him.

"We need string," he barked at the table of still sitting agents. He had little use for them and great disdain. What good was their technology if they couldn't see the puzzle as a whole and not just the pieces, he asked himself.

It didn't take long to see that all the women who had disappeared were clustered in the one park near a running path that was easier to see on the large map than on the tablet. It also showed that most of them lived in the area near the campus or the neighborhood Joseph and Mary were assigned to stay during their visit.

Only Mary's and Teri's last locations were away from the park.

"We need to make sure about the running part," Pea said.

She turned to the agents. "Can you people call the families or friends and make sure that the women were runners? We need to discover exactly what time they might have been taken."

Pea then turned back to the board as if she were running the investigation rather than just the sister of one of the victims.

Thomas covered his mouth to stifle a laugh as the agents began spreading throughout the room, each taking files to call and complete Pea's assignments.

"Fucking force of nature," Thomas heard Jonathan laugh and he started to move toward the table when Trey touched his arm.

"Don't. He's not worth it. His career is over. He let this happen. Hell, his incompetence has probably let it go on as long as it has."

Thomas still continued to stare at Jonathan with hatred.

Jonathan, however, knowing that what Trey had said was exactly true, decided to goad Thomas if for no other reason than he had decided he hated Thomas for his devotion to Joseph and his family.

"Hey, I thought you said you'd rip my head off? Where's your bravado now, big man?"

Thomas's body went rigid with anger. The bastard, he thought. This was all his fault, but Thomas held his anger in check and remained next to Trey.

"Well, I should have known you didn't have the balls to follow through on your threat. You couldn't even keep your own woman alive."

Before Thomas could move, Trey was across the room and had knocked Jonathan flat on his ass. The other agents briefly saw what had happened and then looked away. They had no respect for their "boss" anymore.

Pea went to Trey and walked back to the boards with him as he shook his hand where he had punched Jonathan.

"I love you," she whispered so softly that only he could hear. "But leave the asshole alone. As you told Thomas, he's not worth it."

The second part of her sentence she spoke much louder in order for Jonathan and everyone else in the room to hear her. Just before they reached Thomas, she stopped and faced Jonathan who was struggling back to his feet and trying to adjust his suit coat.

"And I'm no 'fucking force of nature', you bastard. I'm just the sister of one of your victims," she said.

The last part, where she called the women his "victims" landed sharply and was more devastating than any blow Trey or Thomas could have rained on him. It was the one thing for which he felt the most guilt. He walked away from everyone and out the door into the afternoon sunlight where he sat down on a bench and stared off into the distant parking lot where Teri had been taken.

He sighed and sat with his hands placed upon the knees of his expensive grey suit. What a fool I am, he thought. Looking back, he could see that everything he had thought was clever and smart was truly and horribly stupid. He ran one hand through his short brown hair and sat up. He straightened his tie and stood.

Yes, he thought. My career is probably over, but I can do better. I can still try to help.

He strode back into the hall and over to where Pea, Thomas, and Trey stood talking.

He held out his hand to them.

"I am deeply sorry for what I've said and done, but I'm not completely useless. Let me help. Joseph did train me in his old methods. Maybe I can help you in some way."

Thomas looked away, unable to even respond to him, but Pea took Jonathan's hand and shook it.

"Thank you. We need to concentrate on Ree now. The rest is past. Here's what we've found out from your people so far," she said and stepped back from the map to show him the points they had plotted.

He was stunned that he had never seen the running connection. It was as if it were the missing piece of a puzzle that had previously been one color and was now made real with colors and shapes he had never noticed.

"Jesus, you were right. How did you make the running connection? We never saw that," he said.

Pea looked to Trey first and then to Thomas. If she told him that her dead daughter and her sister told her in a dream, she decided she would only sound like a lunatic. So she lied.

"The park seemed to be a favorite spot for runners. I wondered if these women, who were young and physically very fit, might be running there on a regular basis. He had to have grabbed them somewhere where others might not be and where he could do it without being observed."

"You had the points plotted on your tablets. I just saw them the way Joseph showed me . . ." she paused and looked to Thomas.

"The way he showed me once before."

Jonathan turned from the map to face Thomas, who stood with his arms folded across his chest as he stared down at Jonathan.

"Thomas, I am truly sorry for what I said about your fiancée. It was cruel and unnecessary. Please accept my apologies," he said and held his hand out to Thomas.

Thomas looked down at the man's soft hands, the hands of a man who never touched anything more than papers and computer keyboards. He took the proffered hand and quickly shook it and dropped it.

"I'm going to go check on Joseph," Thomas said and walked away from them. He would never forgive or like the man. He could not understand how anyone could sacrifice a friend's wife for his own ambitions.

When Thomas entered the darkened classroom, he found Joseph sitting on the sofa staring off into space.

"Joseph, are you okay? Did you sleep at all?"

Joseph smiled slightly and nodded.

"For a while. I was with Mary and we were dancing with Taylor between us in our arms. It was a good dream and then I heard Mary calling to me. Her voice woke me up. I could hear her saying 'Joseph, find me. Find me, Joseph.' And I was awake, but she wasn't here."

Thomas opened the door and waved for Joseph to follow him.

"Come and eat something. You need food, too. And Pea made some progress. She found a link that everyone had missed."

Joseph stood shakily and walked with Thomas back to the hall.

"Pea would see it. Did she sleep, too? Mary must have called to her, too."

Thomas frowned. He did not like to discuss such things. Pea had brought it up once after the Ridge, but he still couldn't admit to himself what he had seen. He had decided that what he had seen there was a result of being beaten. He had not seen Shawnette since then and he believed that she was at peace and that he had only wanted to see her. He believed that most people, when they experienced such events, did so because they were so afraid to face what they had already lost.

Joseph saw the frown and shook his head.

"I know. I didn't believe in such things either until I saw Pea's daughter, especially when she stopped her mother from shooting the man on the ridge."

Thomas stopped short and placed his hand on Joseph's chest.

"Wait, you saw her on the Ridge?"

"Of course, I saw it all. I saw you talking to Shawnette and Alicia tell her mother to put the gun down. But I never talked about it. What good would it have done? We had all been through enough."

Joseph moved past Thomas and entered the hall and went to where the food was placed on one of the tables and began to fill a plate with food. Thomas followed him, trying to process Joseph's affirmation of what he had thought was merely his own imagination.

As Joseph sat down and ate, he studied the progress they had made while he had rested. They had moved forward and made important connections, but they still had not found the one thing they needed most – the knowledge of the name of the man that Teri had most likely died over.

Just as Pea had come to realize, Joseph also knew it to be true. The pretty little brunette who had been so kind to him and Mary, who probably had a family and friends and a lover, who had probably never been unkind to anyone, was most likely dead. And like Pea, he prayed that her death had not been horrible, but unlike Pea, he knew somewhere within himself that Teri's death had probably been worse than anything Pea could imagine.

The one thing they all needed to concentrate on was what Teri died for – who the man he had seen was, where he was, and where he had taken Mary.

Mary, Joseph thought, I'm coming. Hold on. Live. Live for us, for Taylor. I'm coming. I'll find you.

Chapter Sixteen

Raymond Templeton was showering Teri's blood from his body and he watched it wash into the ground from the outside shower head he had put on the side of the cabin. He had wrapped her body in garbage bags and put it in the back of the maintenance van. He would bury angel Eve tonight before he would dispose of the whore's body.

He rubbed his closely cropped hair with heavy castile soap and used a scrub brush to make sure that no trace of the whore remained on him. He could not allow a drop of her blood to contaminate his angels' hallowed ground. He even scrubbed his teeth and flossed bits of the whore's skin from his teeth. No part of her could remain on him.

He could hear one of the angels inside the cabin just as he turned off the water.

He wasn't sure which one it was, but he had distinctly heard the name "Taylor". It had to be either angel Naomi or his Mary. Angel Ruth had not spoken in days. She just stared at him each night that he came to her. She was getting slower at coming up out of the water and he had planned to use the pear on her tonight, but the whore had changed his plans. He would have to clean it thoroughly before using it on Ruth, which meant that her ascension might be delayed at least for another day.

On the night after angel Ruth's pressing, he would begin using the strappado on angel Naomi. He looked forward to the next few days as each one moved him closer to his final ascension with his Mary. Mary, his queen of heaven. He believed that God would be so pleased with his discovery of her. Their ascension together would signal the rapture and the ascension of all righteous souls to heaven.

But the voice and the name "Taylor" gave him pause. Was there something he had missed about angel Naomi? If he had, he would be delayed even further in his appointed time with Mary. Angel Naomi was the next to last of the angels. Once she was gone, there would be no one left for him but Mary.

He dressed quickly in his clean clothes that he had placed on a tree branch nearby. He was buttoning his shirt as he entered the cabin again, the setting sun glowing behind him forming a halo effect around his entire body.

The sudden sight of him in the doorway with the orange and pink glow behind him made Naomi gasp inadvertently and she closed her eyes to avoid looking at him. He walked to face the cots where Naomi and Mary lie motionless.

"Who is Taylor?"

Mary's eyes flew open involuntarily at his mention of her daughter's name. She did not realize he had heard her say Taylor's name when she was trying to explain to Naomi about her daughter and how he was breaking his "covenant" that mandated the women had no children.

"Oh, my Mary," he said and knelt at the foot of her cot. "Was it you who spoke? Who is this 'Taylor' you spoke of?"

She peered down at him and then closed her eyes and became as still as the other women in the room.

Raymond became agitated that Mary did not seem to understand that she had to respond to him. God willed it. He stood and walked over to her. As she was the holiest of all females, she must speak. He touched her face and saw where the collar had marred her throat and he began to weep.

"Forgive me, Mary. I do not intend to harm you. Your presence here gives grace to the angels who surround you. But God has told me I must do everything this way. Please speak."

Mary and Naomi both were shocked by his actions, but Mary was not about to let him gain any more control over her than he already had. She would hold Taylor's name close in her heart until she thought it might save them. And so she kept her eyes closed and did not move or speak.

"You must speak to me, Mary! God sent me a sign. He has revealed his plan to me. You must speak!" He was yelling now. She could feel his hot breath on her face and feel the spittle that flew from his mouth as he spoke.

It was then that he suddenly began to speak gibberish. She had heard of people speaking in tongues and she wondered if this were what it sounded like. But she still did not know if that was what he was doing and so she did not react. She was afraid to do anything but remain quiet.

After what seemed to be minutes of an unending stream of guttural sounds, he finally stopped and began to speak words she understood again.

"If you do not speak to me after I have finished my work this evening, you will cause more whores to suffer the way the one did tonight. God wills you to speak to me and I can brook no dissent. You are holy, but God has tasked me with you and I must know everything."

He still did not look at her as he knelt over Eve's shrouded body that he had wrapped in linen. He lifted Eve's body and carried her out the door, only pausing to kick it closed as he headed out to the resting place of the mortal bodies of his angels.

As he lay his angel Eve in the ground, he cursed the whore Teri again. She had cost him his last blessed moments with one of his angels. He wept as he placed the body in the pit, prayed, and shoveled dirt onto her.

In the cabin, Mary opened her eyes and tried to speak to Naomi.

"Will he kill other women the way he killed Teri?"

Her ability to speak was getting worse from dehydration. She took the earring from her ear and began to suck on it again, but this time little saliva was produced.

She waited for Naomi to respond and became frightened when no words came from her. "Naomi?"

"I'm . . . here. Don't know. I'm dying . . . I think. My tongue won't work. Water. No water today."

Mary listened as Naomi painfully struggled to form her words.

"Water? He gives us water?"

"Yes," Naomi said and then was quiet again. They both could hear the ragged breathing of Ruth and it did not sound good. Mary found that she was crying, but tears were not falling from her eyes. She realized the women had to have water soon. Another day in the heat of the cabin and one or all of them might not make it. She closed her eyes and thought of Joseph and Taylor again and fell asleep whispering their names.

Raymond Templeton spent most of the evening with his tasks. After burying angel Eve, he went to the van where the whore's body was and drove towards the spot in the swamp where he usually disposed of the bodies of those mortal women who did not make it to the pressing, proving to him that they were not of God, but of man.

He began to worry about the wisdom of speaking to Mary as he had. God might become angry with him for yelling at her. He was unsure of what he should do now. He knew that time was drawing close and he was not only fearful of God's wrath, but also of being discovered by those mortals who would not understand his appointed work on this earth.

After pushing the garbage bags with the whore's body into the brackish water, he got back into the van and drove back toward the campus to retrieve his own vehicle. He was thankful that it would still be dark when he parked the van on the street and left in his own car. It was one less clue for anyone to follow.

What he did not realize in the dark of the van that the bags holding Teri's torn body had leaked onto the floor of the van. He had purposely removed the overhead light in the van and that removal, while working in his favor, also hid from him the bloody evidence of his crime.

By the time he had switched vehicles and headed back to his home, the sun was rising on another day and he began to feel exhausted from his work. He was heading into his house when he realized that he had forgotten one of his most important tasks – water for the angels and Mary. Without it, they would die from dehydration and God would punish him for that.

Mary woke to feel Templeton's skeletal fingers in her mouth and she began to gag. He had placed some sort of pad between her lower jaw and the collar, but his fingers in her mouth were somehow worse than the pain of the collar. She could feel the calluses on the tips of his fingers and the nails that were just a little too long.

She panicked at the thought of what else he might do to her with those fingers as his fetid, hot breath assaulted her nostrils. She realized that the air he exhaled smelled of something rotten within him, a stench that was worse than merely bad breath.

"Mary, do not struggle. I will give you water as God gave the Israelites manna from heaven in the morning dew as they wandered in the wilderness. The water will keep you strong. Drink, now."

He placed a metal cup next to her lips and began to slowly pour water in her mouth. She gagged at first and then began to greedily gulp the water as fast as she could.

When he stopped pouring it into her mouth, he was surprised to hear her speak for the first time.

"More" was all she said, but he smiled and rejoiced that she had graced him with her voice. He took another cupful of water and poured it into her mouth. He did this two more times before he stopped.

"My Mary, I can give your mortal body no more. It will reject it. But I will bring it to you again tonight if you will speak again."

Mary stared at the man and wanted to scream in horror. But, she knew that if she did, he might punish her or the other women so all she did was blink her eyes slowly to signify that she understood.

He left smiling then. He placed the bucket and metal cup next to the water spigot outside the cabin and went home to sleep. He hoped to dream of Mary and their ascension and he felt better now. She had spoken. Surely that was a sign that God still approved of his work.

Chapter Seventeen

Fortunately, the campus police found the white maintenance van on the side street where Raymond had left it. They sadly saw the amount of blood in the back of it, including the streaks where it appeared that a body had been dragged from it.

Unfortunately, Raymond had left no traces of his presence in the van. He had been careful to wear gloves when he used the van and had left no sign of whomever the person was who had used it.

Mary had been missing for almost two days now and although her family and law enforcement had continued to work, they finally had to rest. Pea forced the issue with Joseph and was aided in her efforts by Trey and Thomas. Joseph finally agreed to go back to the house where he and Mary were staying, but he would not go into the master bedroom. As the house had three bedrooms, he went into the smallest guestroom and rested there.

Pea, Trey and Thomas were all too tired to do anything other than try to sleep. Thomas laid down on the sofa and said he would sleep there, giving the other guest room to Pea and Trey. Pea found fresh linens and took a pillow and sheets out to Thomas before returning to lie next to Trey.

Her husband had already fallen asleep by the time she returned and she curled her body around his and held on to him, finally falling asleep herself as she began to breathe in unison with his own quiet rhythmic breaths.

She slept for several hours before the dreams began again and she awoke in tears, feeling useless and worthless to her sister. Next to her, Trey still slept soundly. His body had barely moved since she had slipped into the bed next to him.

She carefully extracted herself from him and quietly walked out of the bedroom and into the living room where Thomas, too, was still sleeping. She tiptoed through the room and carefully opened the sliding glass door to the back yard area. The sun had slipped down in the sky and she thought that it was probably getting close to five o'clock.

She circled the pool and headed toward the small waterfall where she placed her hand to feel the water course through her splayed fingers. She took her wet hand and wiped her face and throat with the water. The heat was so oppressive. She prayed that her sister was not in this heat or the sun. She was about to walk back to the house when she noticed two large footprints in the muddied mulch next to the waterfall.

She knelt and stared at them. Whoever had left these prints was big, perhaps taller or larger than Thomas, who was one of the tallest men she had ever known. The man who left these prints was at least 6'5" or 6'6".

Hadn't Joseph said that the man who had stared at Mary at the conference opening was a very tall man? She ran around the pool and back into the house to the room where Trey still slept. She saw her cell phone on the bed table and picked it up and dialed the number for Jonathan.

Though she despised him and blamed him for Ree's abduction, she still had to be calm with him in order to work with him for Ree's sake. When he answered, his voice was gravelly as if he had been asleep. Well, too fucking bad, she thought. He had to accept the blame for this and he had to do the work.

She spoke in a whisper so as not to disturb Trey and told Jonathan of her discovery at the house. Jonathan became alert at once and said that he and a forensic crew would be there as soon as possible.

She ended the call and looked over to her husband who was awake now and had listened to her conversation. He pulled her down next to him and held her as she cried. She was trying so hard to be strong and he knew it was costing her more than she would reveal to anyone else.

He had stopped believing in 'happily ever after' until he met her. His childhood had been so bereft of care or love that he did not believe anyone could be happy. And even with the trauma they had suffered, he may not have believed in that anymore, but he did believe in one thing more than anything else – the love they shared. Everything else paled in comparison.

They stayed there for awhile before rising to wake Thomas and Joseph and tell them what Pea had found and of the impending arrival of the forensic people.

All three of the men wanted to go out to see the footprints, but they stayed behind the glass and stared out at the pool, knowing that their presence out there could contaminate any possible evidence.

It was most frustrating for Joseph, but he stood there without moving even after Jonathan and the forensic crew began working. Pea brought him a sandwich, which he tried to shake off, but she insisted, threatening to have Thomas remove him if he didn't take it and eat. He nodded and took it, but ate without ever taking his eyes off the activities going on outside the house.

After a few hours, Jonathan came into the house and sat down with them. He explained what they had found – the footprints which appeared to be work boots, but little else.

"We're lucky it hasn't rained. We're heading into the rainy season and it's just luck that it's been dry. The footprints are fairly clear and the forensics team seems to think that they can get something from them," he said

"Here's the other news, and Joseph, this may not be good for you to hear, but we found more prints around the house. It looks as if he may have been in the house when you were here. Do you remember anything odd about that afternoon when you got here?"

Joseph leaned back in the Eames chair and placed his hands over his face. What he knew he could not say and it made him physically ill to think of it. The bastard had been in the house when he and Mary had last made love. How, he asked himself, and then he remembered.

"The door. I may have left it unlocked after I brought our luggage in. He might have come in then, but I don't remember anything else."

He leaned forward and gestured with his hands at the door.

"What the hell was I thinking, not locking that damn door?" He stood and began to pace. He kept running his hands through his hair.

"I should have locked it. I should have . . ."

Thomas stood to calm his friend down.

"Joseph, you can't do this. Mary's still out there. We need you. She needs you. Sit."

Pea clasped Trey's hand in hers so tightly that he thought she would break it, but he didn't speak. She looked so calm on the surface, but he knew she was more terrified than she had ever been.

"You know," she said. "We've been through a lot. And, and we, well, at least I have, always think about all the things we could have done differently or the things we would do differently if something were to happen again. But, you know, you can't plan for this."

She dropped Trey's hand and headed back through the house to where the bedrooms were. Trey watched her and thought about following her, but decided to let her have some time to herself before he went to her.

"So, where do we go from here?" he asked Jonathan.

Jonathan did not know what to say. They were doing everything they could. Now he had to give them more bad news.

"There's more. Joseph, please sit down. We found a maintenance van near campus. The back of it was . . . it was very bloody."

He held his hand up before any of them could speak.

"It wasn't Mary's blood. There's no evidence that Mary was ever in it."

"It was Teri's blood, wasn't it?" Joseph said, shaking his head. He had known Teri was dead. She was expendable in this maniac's plan simply because she had never been part of it and she knew something the killer did not want her to reveal.

Jonathan nodded and looked outside the wall of glass at the crew who were still working even as dusk began to fall. Another night and they had little more than they did when Mary had been taken.

"I want to go back to the conference hall. I've had some rest and I want to look at everything again, especially those employee records," Joseph said.

"Of course," Jonathan replied. "I'll let you guys get yourselves pulled together and we'll head over there."

Thomas looked to Trey and simply nodded his head. Trey stood and went in search of his wife. Another long night for them. Then he thought of Mary and had to stop in the hall for a moment to take a second to think about what she might be going through right now.

How can I even think about it being a long night, he thought, when God only knows what kind of night it might be for her?

Chapter Eighteen

Mary had slept through most of the day. The water the skeleton man had given her had helped. But now she could see the gathering dusk outside and she knew it would not be long before he returned. She realized that he had not removed the padding from between her throat and the collar and she was able to turn her head slightly.

In the dim light she could barely see Naomi, but she could see that he had left the collar unpadded on her. Why is he treating me differently, she asked herself. Then she thought once more about Taylor. She wondered what her baby was doing right now. Was she playing? Did she miss her mommy? Would she remember her mommy when she grew up?

She felt tears on her face this time because she realized for the first time that she might never see her baby or Joseph again. She sobbed and thought of all that she might miss.

No, no, no. I'm not going to think about that. Joseph will find me. I will not give up.

She raised her hands and wiped her eyes and face. She would not give the bastard the satisfaction of seeing that she had cried.

She felt the earring about to tumble from her ear and she barely got her hand to it before it almost fell out and she would have lost it. She started working at the lock again, wishing that she had had Joseph teach her how to pick locks.

What was I thinking, hiding out at Pea's the last few years, she asked herself. She thought of the person she had been before Manley and she grew angry at him, at herself, even at her sister for not seeing or admitting that she saw Manley for the bastard that he was.

Had he not returned to their lives, she would have gone on to have a normal life with Joseph, not one where it seemed as if killers lurked in every corner. By the time darkness had fallen, she had worked herself into such an angry frame of mind that she felt nothing but hate.

Where were her smart sister and brilliant husband now? Why hadn't they found her? Why was she the one raped by her sister's ex-husband? Why had Pea even brought the bastard into their home?

As her anger grew, she became more irrational and was ready to scream curses at Joseph and Pea and Thomas for ever beginning that first search that left her chained in another cabin.

It was only when she saw a light coming toward the cabin through the cracks in the walls that reason began to return to her. She knew by the dim light moving toward the cabin that he was returning. She knew that she needed to stall for time, not just for herself, but for the other women.

She wondered if she spoke to him of God and his beliefs if he would back away from any plans he might have for them that night. She was thinking of what she might say, what religious aphorisms might work, when she heard the water running outside and knew he was bringing it to them. Somehow all she could think of the Gloria Patri her family had sung in the Presbyterian church she had attended growing up and she did not think that singing that would do any of them any good.

The door opened and he entered the cabin carrying a lantern and the bucket of water. He walked to her first, but she did something that surprised even herself. She pointed at the other women in the room, but did not speak.

"You want me to water them first?"

She closed her eyes in disgust at the way he talked about the two women as if they were animals.

'*Water them?*' It took all her strength not to curse at him and just maintain a placid and calm look on her face.

He went to Ruth first, but gave Ruth very little and that worried Mary. She was afraid of what he had planned for Ruth. He gave Naomi two cups and then he came to her side and before he could touch her mouth with those boney fingers, she opened her mouth for the water. He gave her four cups and again she could not fathom why he was treating her differently.

"You said you'd speak if I brought you more water," he said.

"Thank you," Mary said, almost choking on the words, but noticing that his face lit up when she said them to him.

He began to quote scripture again and walked over to Ruth and began to lift her from the bed, heading toward the center post in the cabin.

Mary realized he was going to put Ruth into the leather contraption and knew she had to say something or do something to stop him. Otherwise, he would kill Ruth for sure.

"Please," she said. "Don't. She's too weak. God would not want it, would he?"

Raymond stopped and stared at her and then continued with his work.

"You must not ask me that. This has been decreed by God to happen at this time. All will be revealed at the ascension."

"No," she called out as loudly as she could with her voice broken and the tight collar muting the strength of her voice.

He shook his head and backed away from her, but did not stop what he had started.

For the first time, Ruth could see her face and she stared at Mary in sorrow.

"Thank you," she whispered.

Raymond jumped back in anger, simultaneously pushing Ruth against the pole with his long, thin arm.

"You are not to speak to her. She is above you and your only purpose is to serve her in this life and the next."

Mary covered her eyes with hands. What lunacy was this? This man was implacable. There was nothing she could do to stop his torture of Ruth and she began to openly weep.

Her weeping began to distress Raymond a great deal. Perhaps he was wrong in his plans now, including the use of the pear now. Perhaps the pressing was what God was having his Mary tell him that was all that needed to be done.

"Stop that. Stop that now. Why can't I do this as I have been told to do so before you came? Does our father wish me to do something else? Talk to me! Tell me what to do! Speak!"

His body was still bowed over Ruth's form where he had been placing her in the strappado.

"What did God want of him," he asked as he looked upwards.

"God does not want this," Mary managed to get out of mouth. She did not know what else to say.

"Then what does he want? Am I to press her? What do I do?" he asked Mary.

Mary could not speak. What did he mean 'press her.' Why was she the one he chose to decide the fate of the others? She began to weep again. Before he could turn away to leave, he heard her voice again.

"Taylor," he heard her say.

He rushed to her side and stared into her eyes.

"That name again. Who is he? Am I supposed to find him? Who is he?"

Mary began to panic. Oh god, no. He couldn't go looking for Taylor.

"No, no, no, no, no, no!!" she cried.

From the center of the room, she heard Ruth's voice whisper.

"Me. You are to take me. God . . . has willed it."

Ruth had heard Mary tell Naomi of her daughter and she knew this madman could not go after Mary's child. Besides, she reasoned, I will not live through this night anyway.

"No, Ruth, no," Mary continued to cry.

Ruth simply said, "God has willed it," and was silent.

Raymond nodded and went back to work. "As you say, angel Ruth, I will do. Please tell God when you ascend that I do everything to honor him."

He hoisted Ruth upwards and began first her rape, and then inserted the pear. She bit her tongue into two pieces trying not to scream through the gag as the metal blades of the pear opened and spun around inside her. Blood poured from the corners of her mouth and from between her legs. She passed out as he removed it from with her and the blades sliced away her womanhood.

He then took the water that was left in the bucket and washed her body with it. He took her body down, wrapped it, and left the cabin carrying her gently.

Mary could do nothing but cry and next to her Naomi laid quietly in contemplation of her own fate. Everything that any of the women had every dreamed of was disappearing in this man's religious fanaticism.

Outside, Ruth regained consciousness as Raymond placed the board and first two stones on her body. He removed the gag and the lower tip of her tongue fell out of her mouth with the blood soaked rag.

"Oh angel Ruth, I am so very sorry. Your face and mouth were not to be damaged. Can you say anything?" He wiped the blood from her face as he spoke.

Ruth, who had been running in the park when she had tripped into hell, was a graduate student in education. She had been a beautiful, vibrant woman who had known since she was young that she wanted to teach. She had a fiancée, parents and siblings, and the promise of a job in the rural Georgia county where she had grown up. Outside of Macon, Georgia, near her home, she had only travelled to Atlanta and Orlando.

She knew now, with the weight of the stones on her body, the broken limbs, the blood that poured out of her, the dehydration and the loss of part of her tongue, that she would never see the kindergarten room that waited for her in the farmland country outside Macon. She closed her eyes and refused this monster his last request. She would die on her terms, but her torment at last would be over.

Growing up in a southern Baptist church, she had never conceived that such a mad man would warp the words she treasured and believed so strongly. She did not understand God's purpose in her dying this way, but she still held tight to her faith. The monster's voice became noise that she refused to hear. Instead, she began to recite the Lord's Prayer in her head, asking God to forgive her for her sins and her moments of doubt.

Of all the women that Raymond had brought to the cabin, she had been the first virgin, although he had not known this. When he raped her earlier, he did not know that the tears that rained down from her face onto him were for her loss of her purity, her loss of a wedding night, her loss of any future.

When he did not hear her speak after he removed the gag, he waited for a few minutes sitting next to her for a sign from God. When no sign came, he stood and began to move the stones from the wall to her body. It did not take long for her breathing to reach the point where he knew her ascension was imminent.

He placed one last stone on her chest, stripped himself of his clothing, and sat nude in the moonlight next to her face and waited.

As her final breath weakly escaped her swollen lips, he placed his mouth over hers and sucked the last of the air out of her lungs. She struggled only slightly, by now completely unaware of whom she was or what was happening to her.

He began to expiate the poisons from his body while he covered her mouth. He stroked himself over and over, but he could not find release. He became frustrated and took her dead hand that had fallen loose from the cloth and the stones and placed it under his and tried to use it to assist him, but still nothing happened.

He worked for what seemed like an hour trying to release the poisons, even using her blood as a lubricant and nothing he did worked.

He began to howl at the heavens. Angel Ruth could not ascend without this final release. This was his second failure in releasing an angel to God.

His Mary had been right. God had not wanted this. Why had angel Ruth lied to him, saying that God willed it? He saw that it was his arrogance that had made him ignore Mary's pleas.

He sat with his erect, but useless penis and Ruth's dead hand in his hands. He had wasted this opportunity and God was angry with him. He could feel the poisons build his erection, but he knew that God's punishment was that he carry them because of his failure to listen.

There was something else he thought as he sat there, something he had missed. It was that name – Taylor. He would not have heard Mary say it if it did not mean something to the rapture.

Without thinking, he dropped Ruth's hand and ran back through the woods to the cabin. He burst into the room, naked, with his penis fully erect. Both Naomi and Mary, who had not heard him coming, were terrified when the door flew open and he entered, his skeletal form covered in blood and his penis aimed at them, his face in a grimace of pain and confusion.

"Who is Taylor? God wills that you tell me!"

Chapter Nineteen

Joseph, Pea, Trey and Thomas sat at tables still standing in the conference hall, each with a stack of employee folders they were reading, looking for any man who might resemble the man Joseph had seen staring at Mary the first afternoon they were there.

The FBI agents had already gone through each of the folders and had separated the female employees from the males so that the quartet only had to go through part of the campus staff.

The bureau had actually gone beyond the maintenance people and had included professors, administrators, graduate assistants, and even work study students. When

Joseph saw the stacks of folders that remained after he had worked through many of them, he threw up his hands in anger, stood and kicked the chair in which he had been sitting across the room.

"Fuck this! The man was too old to be a student and he wasn't a teacher. Why are we looking at files that are a waste of time?"

He started to walk away from the table, stopped, sighed, and then picked up the chair and reseated himself at his table, opening a new file.

Pea looked to Trey and Thomas at their tables and then went back to the file folders in front of her. She had thought the same thing an hour ago, but she and the others had been assured by the HR people who had provided the folders that all the files were important, and after all, the school did have older students, too.

She held her hand over one of the stacks and closed her eyes, trying to imagine where Ree might be, who might be with her. She shook her head and looked up at the clock. Ten-thirty. Forty-eight hours plus since Ree had gone into that bathroom.

Pea turned around and tried to imagine the room full of people, her beautiful, fragile sister standing next to

Joseph, then leaving his side and walking to the hall exit. Unconsciously, Pea stood as if to follow her sister through the hall doors, into the building and toward the Ladies room.

She paused outside the Ladies room door and placed her hand on it the way she had on the stack of files. Nothing. She looked to her left and right and wondered if anyone had been near Ree at that second.

Pea entered the restroom and stood in the center of the small area, opening each stall and looking at areas the forensic team had already covered. When she exited the last stall, she looked around the room again. No windows. No vents large enough for a person. Nothing but the counter, sinks and a long mirror.

She walked to the mirror and stared at her own reflection, watching it morph into her sister's face, her blonde hair becoming red, her white blouse becoming a black lace dress that ironically Ree had borrowed from her sister.

Suddenly, her sister's face disappeared and all she saw was her own reflection. She bent over the sink and felt ill. She fought to keep the tears from falling, fought not to admit that her sister might be gone forever, fought not to admit that they might never know what had happened to Ree.

What then? How long did they do this before they returned home, Joseph alone, without his wife to a daughter who would soon forget her mother's voice, the way Ree laughed, the smell of her hair and skin?

That was when Pea broke. She thought of her own boys growing up that way, of Trey growing up without his own mother, and she fell into a heap in the floor, hugging her knees and wailing like a lost child.

Unknown to her, her cries were heard by everyone in the hall. Trey heard his wife's cry first and sprinted in the direction it came from. Thomas and Joseph were at his heels, followed by the other people working on Mary's disappearance.

Trey followed the sound to the Ladies room and threw open door to see his wife sitting in the floor, a pathetic, crumpled figure. He rushed to her and knelt to hold her as she continued to wail.

Thomas and Joseph, who saw that Pea was safe and that Trey was with her, barricaded the door from the prying eyes of the others, letting them know that everything was okay and that it was a family matter. The others slowly filed away and back into the hall except for Jonathan who stood some distance from the men.

"Is she okay?" he asked.

Before Joseph could stop him, Thomas had Jonathan slammed against the wall, pinning him there by his shirt collar. Surprisingly, Jonathan did nothing to fight back.

"Thomas," Joseph said. "Thomas! Let him go. Just let him go."

Thomas released Jonathan, but did not move thus not allowing Jonathan passage.

"Come on, let's get back to those damn files," Joseph said and Thomas reluctantly followed him.

Inside the bathroom, Trey held Pea until her tears finally stopped, until her body stopped shaking, and she leaned against him, limp and spent. Neither of them said a word, but continued to sit together for another 10 minutes.

At last, Trey stood and held his hand out to Pea, who took it and raised herself from the floor. The two of them walked from the restroom, both still silent. Just as they turned toward the hall and away from the Ladies room, Pea saw something glint out of the corner of her eye.

She stopped and turned to look in the opposite direction. Nothing but two large silk fig trees. She tilted her head and saw the glint again. This time she walked to the trees and looked closely at them. She had seen something in those leaves.

She stuck her hand into the branches and examined the leaves for anything that did not seem right. Suddenly her hand touched plastic and metal and she pulled it from within the tree.

It was an employee name badge with a picture. A picture of a man in his forties, very skinny, with slicked back hair that touched just below his collar, the collar of a grayish maintenance uniform. A name was boldly printed across the bottom of the badge: Raymond Templeton.

Pea's hand began to shake violently.

Could it be? Could this be?

Her mind was going in a thousand directions, but she believed that she had just found the key to where Ree might be. God, please, she prayed. Let this be what we need. Let us find Ree.

She ran to Trey and handed the badge to him. He took one look at it, looked at her and smiled and grabbed her hand, pulling her behind him as he ran back into the conference hall.

"Pea found something!" he said excitedly.

"I think this may be the person we're looking for," he said as he reached Joseph's table and laid the badge on the table.

Joseph sat stunned for a moment before speaking.

"That's him! That's the man I saw and we have his name now. Everyone, look through your folders and see if you can find him. His folder should have his address and everything we need to find him."

Everyone in the room scrambled to the four tables and began going through the stacks of folders looking for one that had the name 'Raymond Templeton' on it. After thirty minutes, no one could find the folder, which unbeknownst to them, Raymond had removed before taking Teri in the parking lot.

"It's not here," Trey said from his table. The other people at the other tables responded in kind.

Joseph looked to one of the campus police officers helping, handed him the badge and asked him if the badge was real or if it could have been counterfeited.

The officer, who had done little more than fetch meals or files for the others in the room, studied the badge carefully. He was not stupid, but he did not want to make a mistake about this so he was slow in replying to Joseph's query. He turned the badge over several times, looked at every aspect of it, from the size to the colors used and the holographic seal of the university embedded on it.

Everyone in the room was looking at him, waiting for his response, and he felt the weight of the woman's life on his shoulders.

"Yes," he said. "I believe it's real. I've seen hundreds of these, but I've never seen one counterfeited. See, the holographic seal? That would make it very hard to fake."

Joseph took the badge back and stared at it. They had a face and name, but no file to match it. Even if the guy had been a temporary hire, the HR people should have had a file or something on the guy. There had to be a trace unless . . .

Joseph stood up and called across the room to the one man who had kept working on the employee database rather than joining the folder search.

"Uh, Ted? Ted, if the guy had somehow pulled his folder from the HR department, would he have been able to erase his records from the computer system?"

He walked over to where Ted had spent the past few days going through the employee and student database without much success. The vague description Joseph had given him had been of little help. There were so many people that "tall, skinny, white man in a maintenance uniform" had not given him much with which to work. But now, now they not only had a name, they might have more.

"Does it have an employee ID number on it?" he asked Joseph.

"Yes, here it is. See if he's in the system," Joseph said.

Ted typed the name and number into the search parameters he had set up. No such name or number found.

"That doesn't make sense," Ted said, holding the card and studying it as the campus officer had. "There should be at least the number in the system. See, there are numbers issued before it and ones after . . . Ah, shit. Why didn't I think of that?"

He looked up to Joseph and did not want to say what Joseph and the others were already thinking.

"He not only pulled his file. He erased his existence from the computer," Joseph said and sat down next to Ted.

Ted nodded and continued to look at the badge.

"You know, that's fairly high tech for a janitor. I don't think this man was just a janitor. Maybe he was hiding in plain sight – a predator who found his prey by being invisible to everyone around him," Ted said.

"Yeah, that would give him an excellent feeding ground," one of the other agents said and Joseph winced.

Before anyone could speak, Jonathan spoke to the agent, who silently left the room.

Joseph shook his head.

"Stop him, Jonathan. He was only saying what we were all thinking, no matter how painful. You need to get control of yourself before jumping on them."

The agent returned and apologized to Joseph, who simply waved him away and turned back to Ted at his laptop.

"Ted, he might have erased himself from the system, but what about back-ups? Surely a system this big has back-ups of some sort," Joseph said.

"Of course," Ted said and began typing wildly, trying to access the most recent back-up before the conference.

After a few minutes, he said "Aha!"

"Raymond Templeton. Maintenance employee for the past eight years. Some references that don't look too kosher. Shit, the fool had a 401K and insurance, though. He thought he was being smart, but not that smart."

"For God's sake," Joseph cried, "What his address? Save the rest for prosecuting the bastard. I need to know where to find him!"

Ted gave Joseph the Christmas, Florida address, but before Joseph, Pea, Trey and Thomas could leave, Jonathan stepped in front of them.

"Joseph, you can't go. You know that. You have to let us handle this."

Joseph stared at the agent with contempt.

"Try and fucking stop us. You have no right to keep us here. And you have to get a warrant. I don't need that. I'm not with the bureau anymore," he said and pushed past Jonathan, followed by his friends.

"Joseph, stop!" Jonathan called out uselessly.

Shit, he thought and turned to one of the Florida State Patrol officers.

"How soon can you get a warrant? They could be walking into something more than they can handle. Who knows what this guy has done. He might even be innocent."

The agent that Jonathan had told to leave, said "Yeah, right" and walked out of the hall this time, his disgust with his 'boss' plain for everyone else to see.

Chapter Twenty

It was well after midnight by the time they neared Christmas. Joseph had tried to program the address into the rental car's navigation system, but without success. It kept coming up "No such street."

They were driving through dark streets when Pea spied a McDonald's still open.

"There, Joseph. Pull in that McDonald's. I can run in and ask if anyone there knows where this road is."

Joseph swerved across the median and pulled into the lot of the restaurant. Pea dashed from the car inside the well lit restaurant. Trey thought for a second that there was almost a brilliant clarity that shone from within the restaurant that seemed to promise the hope of finding Mary.

They watched as she spoke to the night shift employees, holding the paper with Templeton's address on it to them. They could see the people shaking their heads and their spirits sank. Then suddenly an older man came out into the bright light of the McDonald's dining room. He looked at the address, nodded and began pointing, talking to Pea. Some of the others in the McDonald's, nodded as well and they, too, then pointed in the same direction.

It seemed to Joseph as if Pea were in there forever, but she had only been gone for five or six minutes before she was jumping back into the car.

"The kids didn't recognize the road at first because some of the road names have been changed in the last 20 years. But the older man, he knew it. He said he went to church that way and that the address was an old farmstead on the way to his church."

"Just tell me which way to go. The sooner we get there, the better," Joseph said and they headed out to Old Templeton Road, where the Templeton Orchards used to be, but now was a housing development with new county road numbers and few names. The old Templeton place and the church were the only places that still used the Templeton Road address anymore, the older man had said.

As Joseph and his group headed to the Templeton farm, as Jonathan paced the floor waiting for a warrant for Templeton's house, Raymond Templeton had turned his wrath on Naomi. He had to have answers or God would punish him further.

He began to beat her naked body with a riding crop while he continued to stare at Mary and demanded to know who Taylor was. He ignored Naomi's struggles to protect her breasts and belly, her screams that caused the collar to dig into her throat and the base of her neck.

"Tell me now! Tell me! God has willed this. The rapture must come and you and the angels are the key to it. I have found many a whore of Babylon in my search and I have found angels whose ascension brought you to me. God's work must be done. He has told me this," he said and slashed open the skin on the side of Naomi's breast as he struck her again with the riding crop.

"Stop, please. Stop," Mary cried.

"Tell me and she shall be released. Tell me now! I have lost two angels because of your appearance. God's plan can only be revealed through you now."

Mary watched the horror of the nude, blood covered man whose erection grew with each lash he placed on Naomi's body. Disgust filled her. God had nothing to do with his plans, she thought, only his sick and twisted sexual needs disguised by a religion he had created wholly.

"Ruth is dead? What did you do to her? Where is she?"

Templeton hit Naomi again with the crop, this time cutting across her bare legs. Mary did not know how much longer Naomi could last through the beating.

"Angel Ruth has been pressed with the stones, but she cannot ascend until the poisons have been released from my human form and that is not happening because of you. Tell me or I will do more to this angel!"

His voice was nearly hysterical as he tried to coerce Mary to reveal who Taylor was. While Mary continued to weep and begged him to stop, she watched as he removed Naomi's collar and started to lift her from the bed. Naomi, who still had the full use of her limbs, began to fight Templeton, beating at him and reaching her fingers to his eyes, intent on gouging them and blinding him. As she did this she also kicked at his groin, but Ruth's blood mixed with her own from the beating and the sweat on both their bodies made it impossible for her to gain a purchase on his body.

While he was unprepared for her sudden onslaught and the strength she still had, he used his size against her. He kneed her hard in the gut and then grabbed both her hands and started to crush her long fingers with his much larger hands.

Naomi screamed from the pain as her hands were crushed, but continued to struggle against his hold on her. She knew what would happen to her if he put her in the leather straps. She would be as dead as Eve and Ruth. Her adrenalin fueled her body and she hurled herself and Raymond onto the floor where she scrambled to stand and kick him as hard as she could. Her body was weak, but she fought with the ferocity she needed to survive.

She was so close to success as he began to try to roll away from her that she began to look around the room for something to hit him with other than her kicks. And that brief second of inattention brought her down as Templeton did see a weapon. Under Mary's cot next to where he cowered, he saw the dim shape of an old tire iron.

He grabbed it and swung it out at Naomi's ankles, shattering the right one and sweeping both legs out from under her. In his rage at her rebellion, he began to beat her with the tire iron the way he had with the riding crop. It was only Mary's screams that stopped him from killing Naomi.

Naomi was now broken and pliable to his will. While she could barely move her body, her mind still worked. She was awake and felt every pain as he placed her in the center of the room to begin to lift her with the leather device.

"I will use the strappado and the pear now, if you don't tell me who this Taylor is," he said to Mary.

Mary could see the wild look of fear and then agony as Naomi was hoisted into the air with what the skeleton man had called the "strappado". He raised her just enough to insert himself into her and he began to quote scripture again that devolved into what Mary thought of as his talking in tongues as he raped Naomi. He did this for at least ten minutes before removing himself from her and still finding his penis erect.

He punched Naomi's belly in frustration and left her hanging and moved to Mary's side, his bloody penis almost in her face.

She tried to wriggle away from him, but the collar made it impossible. All she could do was put her hands up between him and her face, trying not to think of what he might do next in his religious fervor to "relieve" himself of the "poisons" he had said had infected him.

"You are sick. God will damn you to hell," she cried. "You use God as an excuse to rape and murder women. Your . . . your rules on the walls, the schedule of torture . . .

"Get away from me!" she screamed at him. "You are a foul and sick man. Leave us alone!"

He knelt at the side of her bed as if in reverence, but his words belied any reverence he might have once had for her as a being sent to him by God. He smiled as he spoke.

"I will kill her and then you and I will find this Taylor and kill him as well. You may be a harlot sent by Satan to fool me and you will not be pressed, but I will burn you, witch. And I'll find that sister of yours and burn her as well. Even that man you whored yourself to while I listened," he said softly.

Mary's eyes widened in fear at his disclosure of everything he did know, including that she and Joseph had made love late in the afternoon before the conference opening ceremony.

"Yes, my Mary, I was in your house and I heard the sound of his fornication with you. I know you are bound to him in your mortal form as his wife, but I will know whether you are from God or a whore from Satan."

He stood and walked back to Naomi and looked back to Mary.

"Satan could have sent you to stop the ascension of my angels. Only you can stop this angel's pain by telling me the truth."

He then moved back to Naomi and pushed himself into her again. He raised Naomi's legs and pulled her body down onto his. With every movement, the strappado tore at her arms and hurt her more than the rape ever could physically.

Mary began to think that he could not climax, that his erection would not end and she saw that Naomi's struggles with the strappado might cause her death after the beating he had given Naomi with the tire iron.

"I'll tell you. Let her down. Stop and I'll tell you," she said.

Templeton stopped and smiled at her, thrust himself one more time into Naomi, and then lowered Naomi from the strappado, rolling her torn body across the floor like a broken toy.

"Of course, of course. You'll tell me because you're going to take angel Naomi's place. Maybe God or Satan will speak to you then," he said.

Mary was about to scream as he shoved the rag into her mouth and lifted her to the floor next to Naomi's bleeding body. She felt the weight of the collar pulling against her neck and she barely stopped her neck from breaking by using both hands to support the collar as he put her into the floor next to Naomi.

Mary looked around frantically and saw that Naomi was still alive and watching Mary being put into the device.

"Tell him," she whispered. "Tell him and live," she said and closed her eyes.

Chapter Twenty-One

Mary's family arrived at Raymond Templeton's house almost an hour after their stop at the McDonald's. They had gotten lost twice in the developments surrounding his farm before they finally saw an old sign that said 'Templeton Road'.

As they approached the house, Joseph turned the headlights off and slowly drove up Templeton's driveway. There were lights on in the house, but they could see no movement.

"Shit," Joseph said. "I wish we had a gun. We don't know what we're walking into."

He felt so frustrated. He knew they were so close to Mary. He could feel that she was here. And he didn't know how to get into the house to find her.

"Maybe we should walk around the house and see if he's in there first," Trey said.

"Sounds better than sitting here," Thomas said and he opened the back car door. Trey was reminded of the last time Thomas had charged forward from a dark car. He had almost died from the gunshot that Manley had inflicted on him.

Trey, Pea and Joseph got out and followed Thomas as he crept around the south side of the house. Other than the light from the house the land around the farm was completely dark. Clouds obscured the night sky and not even starlight lit their way.

"Be very careful," Trey whispered. "He could have set traps. You don't want to get shot again."

Thomas nodded and led them around the house. They could see into the rooms. Everything inside the house looked normal, except for what Pea thought seemed to be an inordinate amount of religious portraits, crosses, and crucifixes on the walls in almost every room.

"Do you guys see the religious stuff?" she whispered.

They nodded in unison and continued around to the back of the house. As they neared the swimming pool, they all stopped as one. Across from them on the far side of the swimming pool, they could see the body of a woman with red hair under the enormous burden of huge stones weighing on her body. An large pool of blood circled her body and her face was turned away from them. Before anyone could speak, Pea ran forward.

No, she thought, this can't be Ree, please God, no.

As she turned Ruth's face toward her, she almost fell backward with relief that it was not her sister's dead body lying at her feet.

"Oh, sweet Jesus, what has he done to this woman?"

Trey moved closer to Pea and the woman.

"I recognize her. Her picture was on the board. She disappeared from the park about three weeks ago. I think her name was Ruth."

Joseph touched Ruth's cheek and felt the warmth that her body still held.

"She hasn't been dead long. Maybe an hour at most. Which means that Mary may still be here somewhere. She may still be alive," he said.

"Why would he kill her this way?" Pea asked Joseph.

"I'm not sure." His desperation was making it difficult for him to think straight.

"This used to be a way the Inquisition killed witches. I think it was called 'Pressing'. It certainly looks like that's what he did here. Though the amount of blood makes me think there might be worse wounds under the weight of the stones."

He could hear the detachment in his voice and he knew it was some effort to keep from thinking of his wife being tortured.

"Oh my god, Joseph, I can't . . . we've got. Ree, oh God, if he has tortured her," Pea said.

"Don't. Don't go there. We've got to find her."

While Thomas went to look in the windows of the house once more and Pea and Joseph examined the woman who had been crushed by the stones, Trey found a trail of bloody footprints that faded into the woods beyond the woman's body.

"Hey, come look," Trey hissed at them.

They moved to where the bloody footprints disappeared into the woods. The was a small path that they could discern, but once again, their ignorance of what lay ahead gave them pause.

"Pea, stay here with Joseph. Thomas and I will follow the trail. We can't chance him grabbing you and Joseph . . . Joseph, your health. Ree will need you to be here." Trey said.

"Trey, please be careful. Please. Thomas, both of you watch out for each other." Pea pleaded.

Trey stopped and walked back to her and kissed her. He placed his hands on each side of her head and stroked her blonde hair as he spoke.

"No matter what happens, I love you. Remember that. I waited so long for you and you, you rescued me. You taught me to be brave. If things go bad, if . . . run. Go to our boys. And know that I will love you forever."

"No, don't say that. No, no, you can't leave me here. You can't leave . . ."

Pea began to weep and leaned against Joseph, who hugged her and used the hug to restrain her from following her husband who followed Thomas with a flashlight.

As the two men disappeared into the darkness of the trail until the flashlight was like a firefly in the night, Pea fell to her knees. She had no idea that she was kneeling in the same spot that Raymond Templeton had knelt and seen the shooting star the evening he had formed his plan and had taken Mary.

She, too, looked up at the sky and prayed wordlessly for the safety of the people she loved. She could not imagine her life without any of them. They had been through so much together. Why had their lives been moved in this direction? Did such great love demand such great sacrifices, she asked.

Joseph paced back and forth to her side, watching the woods. He felt as if he were coming undone by being a bystander at the most important moment of his life.

"Pea, I can't stay here. I have to be there if Mary's there. I have to go to her," he said.

She stood and took his hand and nodded her head.

"Lead the way," she said.

Chapter Twenty-Two

Naomi, who lie broken and bleeding on the floor of the cabin, watched as Mary was hoisted into the air with the strappado. Naomi was on her back, unable to move either her arms or legs. She thought that both her arms were broken, but she had been spared the Pear. She closed her eyes, unable to watch as the man began his torture of Mary.

Unlike the others, he secured Mary in the leather straps before removing the collar. He did not lift her very far in the air. She was able to support some of her weight of her feet, but she didn't know how long her toes could take the position she was in. She knew that if she left the ground that her arms would be torn backward if she were lifted up.

He removed the rag from her mouth.

"Will you talk to me now, my Mary? Will the strappado rip your arms from their sockets or will God deliver you? For Satan, if he be your master, will laugh at your pain."

Mary could barely breathe and she struggled to speak from the pain that was beginning to burn in her arms and legs.

"You," she whispered. "You cannot do this. You are breaking the rules God has given to you."

He stared at her as if she were unlike anything he had ever seen before.

"How can you know about the rules God gave me?"

She closed her eyes tightly. God give me strength, she thought.

"The writing on the walls. I read it. You missed one. . . you missed one with me."

He looked to the walls and then back to her.

"I missed nothing."

"You did. I . . . I have a child. You have broken God's rules by taking me."

His face became as crimson as his blood streaked body. He jumped around the cabin and pointed at the walls and danced wildly back to her.

"Take that lie back! You do not have a child! You are Satan's whore! God would not have me break his rules!"

Mary took a deep breath. She thought that this might be her last chance.

"God gave me a child. Taylor. God blessed me and if you do this . . . you have cursed yourself. God will send avenging angels."

"You lie!" he yelled and without placing the gag in her mouth, lifted her legs into the air, wrapped them around him and pushed himself into her, simultaneously pulling her down. He would release his poisons into her now, he thought. She was a harlot sent by Satan to tempt him. He would throw her in the swamp and he would press angel Naomi and continue his search for the real Mary.

But without the rag in her mouth, she issued a piercing scream into the humid night air as her arms were being torn from her back.

Thomas and Trey had just found the cabin as Mary's scream cut through the quiet night. They recognized her voice and they suddenly felt chill in the humid, hot air.

Behind them, not more than a hundred yards away, Joseph and Pea heard the scream as well and they began to run in the direction of the sound of Mary's agony.

Just as Templeton began to rape Mary, whom he now saw as sent by Satan, a whore on whom he would use the tests to punish, the door of the cabin flew open and Thomas's great muscular body filled the door of the cabin.

Templeton froze and thought that he saw wings spread across the wall of the cabin from the light of Trey's flashlight that backlit Thomas and almost blinded Raymond. He thought Thomas was Gabriel, sent from God to punish him as Mary said. When Trey entered behind Thomas, Trey appeared to Templeton as an angel as well — the Archangel Michael.

Raymond Templeton withdrew his flaccid penis from Mary and knelt before the men he thought were archangels and began to beg their forgiveness as Mary continued to scream from being hung in the strappado.

As Thomas rushed to release Mary from her hanging position, Joseph and Pea reached the door just as Thomas released her, holding her in his arms, supporting her body the way he had supported Taylor's head the first time he had held her the day she was born. He was carrying Mary towards Trey when Templeton saw Joseph and Pea and realized that he had been duped, that these men were not archangels, but just mortals.

In his rage, he grabbed the tire iron from the floor next to Naomi and rushed after Thomas. Thomas heard the man's movements behind him and stepped aside just as Templeton brought the iron down toward his head.

The iron missed Thomas's head and instead bruised against Mary's face, crushing her cheekbone. Trey had already began moving toward Templeton as he saw him moving to hit Thomas and although Trey was unable to stop the blow from crashing into Mary's face, he threw himself into Templeton, whose strength surprised Trey as the man's skeletal, bloody nude body hid the strength of his madness.

Before Trey could react, Templeton had him on the ground and straddled him, about to bring the tire iron down on Trey's skull. Just as Templeton was about strike, he heard a woman's voice behind him and he paused long enough for Trey to punch Templeton in his groin as hard as he could.

The punch was enough to bring the man down and he fell forward against Trey who pushed Templeton off him.

Trey grabbed the tire iron and began to swing it down over and over against Templeton's head. He did not stop until the man's crushed skull was broken open and grey brain matter clotted his stringy, greasy hair. Templeton's body twitched in its death throes for a few moments and then all movement ceased.

Thomas carried Mary out onto the porch and Joseph ripped his shirt off to wrap Mary's body in it. She had passed out when Thomas lowered her and released her from the strappado.

She moaned as she fought to swim back to consciousness. Her face was cut and broken, her shoulders dislocated, but she managed to see Joseph holding her.

"You found me. I called out to you and you found me," she whispered, leaning her face into his bare chest.

Joseph stroked her head.

"Always. I will always find you."

She blinked repeatedly, trying to get her eyes to focus, the shock, pain and dehydration temporarily making everything seem out of sync. She managed to get one word out – Taylor, before she passed out again. He held her in his arms and rocked her gently, knowing that the worst was over.

Chapter Twenty-Three

In the cabin Thomas went to help Trey and Pea try to help Naomi. Pea grabbed a sheet off the bed and covered Naomi's nude body with it, giving the woman her dignity back for the first time in weeks. Naomi smiled weakly as tears streamed across her face. It would be months before she would walk again, almost a year before her body had completely recuperated, but it would take the rest of her life to put the events of Templeton's torture from her mind. Every second of the time in the cabin would become a movie that constantly played in her mind the rest of her life.

"Mary?" she managed to ask and they assured her that Mary was okay. She, too, then closed her eyes and fell unconscious.

"I need to check Ree," Pea said.

Trey nodded and sat down in the floor next to Naomi. He looked over at Templeton's body. He had always thought that he would do anything to protect Pea, but he never thought that killing another human being might be part of it. Not that he regretted what he had done. But he wondered if that possibility of taking a life had always existed in him, if it existed in everyone.

He wiped his hand across his eyes and rubbed the bridge of his nose. He had truly thought that he would not survive the night. He had thought that he would never see his sons again and when he had kissed Pea before following Thomas into the woods he had believed that he was really saying good-bye to her.

The enormity of what he had done was only balanced by his amazement that he had done it and had managed to keep his family intact.

He looked out the cabin door at Joseph and Mary, with Pea squatting next to them and Thomas standing watch over them, listening to the distant sound of sirens. For a moment he thought that they did look like angels from a Renaissance painting.

Trey checked Naomi and saw that she was blessedly unconscious. He stood and walked out on the porch where his wife moved to stand and put her arm around his waist. Trey looked at Pea and then closed his eyes.

"I couldn't stop. I thought he would rise up and continue to fight me. I just don't know what happened. He just wouldn't stop."

"He's gone, Trey. I'm not sorry. You're alive. We all survived. I just want to go home."

Trey reached out touched her cheek and offered her a small smile.

"Home. What a beautiful word."

Reneé Porter

ABOUT THE AUTHOR

Reneé Porter is the author of the series of novels, **The Taliaferro Chronicles**, including *The 13th Victim* and *Redemption Ridge*, as well as the novels *Bell Park* and *Dreamville*. *An Inquisition of Angels,* volume III of **The Taliaferro Chronicles**, is her fifth novel.